"We could try to sleep standing up."

Greg was half serious. He didn't want to leave Leslie even for a moment, but there was no way they could lie down together without succumbing to temptation. They'd proved that over the past week.

"Wouldn't work." She bit down gently on his bottom lip. "We're so exhausted one of us would collapse and there we'd be, back in a horizontal position."

He groaned and pulled her tightly against him, then with the lightest of kisses released her.

"Good night," she whispered. Her eyes devoured Greg as he crossed the room. Suddenly she didn't care if she never slept again. "Don't go."

He turned, to see her sink down onto the bed. "Actually," he murmured with a smile, "I *was* feeling an attack of insomnia coming on...."

Kate McKenzie is the pen name shared by Catherine Dees and Kay Croissant, close friends and collaborators. From their neighboring houses in Pasadena, Cathy and Kay have originated an impressive number of varied projects. But until the idea for *Bed and Breakfast* was born, this talented and prolific pair hadn't ventured to write a Harlequin Temptation. We're happy they met the challenge because we think you'll enjoy this warm and charming story.

Bed and Breakfast

KATE McKENZIE

Harlequin Books

TORONTO • NEW YORK • LONDON
AMSTERDAM • PARIS • SYDNEY • HAMBURG
STOCKHOLM • ATHENS • TOKYO • MILAN

Published February 1987

ISBN 0-373-25243-9

Printed in Canada

1

THE PHONE RANG for the second time. Leslie rolled over in bed and groped for the bedside lamp, but it wasn't there. Her disorientation lasted only a moment, then she remembered where she was. She lifted the phone from its cradle.

"Leslie?" The male voice on the other end was low and intimate. "Did I wake you?"

Leslie didn't answer for a beat while she fought down a surge of irritation. "It's been a long day, Derek. I went to sleep early."

"I haven't been able to sleep at all, love," he breathed. "I thought you might be thinking what I've been thinking...."

"I was dead to the world," she said cautiously.

"Santa Barbara isn't a place to sleep alone, little one. What do you say? I can be there in two hours and we can talk everything out...but only after I show you how terribly much I've missed you already. What do you say, Leslie?"

Her mind was clearer now. She found the lamp in the strange room, switched it on and checked her travel clock. It was nearly midnight. "You're going back on your promise," she reminded him gently but firmly.

"Good Lord, Leslie, what did you expect? I'm down here in L.A. pacing around like a caged lion while the woman I love is trying to get her head straight in some motel! We both know what you need right now, and it isn't separation, dammit!"

Leslie bristled. "Didn't you hear anything I said today? We're not getting married. I'm not in love with you. If that's being blunt, then maybe that's the best way to be. What we had was...was something else, not love. Derek, I'm too tired to go over it all again. Please..."

A long, exasperated sigh reached her ears. "You'd rather stay in some oceanfront motel for ten days pretending we don't have something terrific between us? Can you lie there in your ridiculous rented bed and swear to me that you don't want me—just a little—or that you wouldn't be responsive if I crawled in next to you tonight? Leslie O'Neill doesn't tell a lie—I know that."

"There's a hell of a lot more to my life than that, Derek Parsons," she shot back. She was sitting upright now, growing more and more annoyed by his slick lawyer's tactics. "And I resent being tracked down like this."

"All right, then. Spend the night in splendid isolation. But don't forget what it could have been like. I'll call you tomorrow morning and I expect a change of heart. Sweet dreams, Leslie."

She slammed down the receiver, feeling frustrated. A long way from returning to sleep now, her nerves frayed, she began to notice things about the room.

There was the stale smell of cigarettes. Cheap oil paintings were bolted to the wall, the garish swirl print of the drapery fabric matched the polyester quilted bedspread. Derek was right, she thought. It was a ridiculous rented bed, just like millions of others. Even the plastic water pitcher and wrapped glasses spoke to her of sameness.

Restless, she pulled back the curtain at the sliding door to the narrow balcony facing the ocean. In the far distance, sparkling like dozens of lighted Christmas trees floating on the water, were massive oil drilling platforms. The citizens of the coastal towns had fought hard to prevent their construction, and earlier today Leslie had thought of the rigs as a blight on an otherwise magnificent expanse of cobalt blue sea. But at night, bathed in the silver glow of an almost full moon, they looked beautiful.

Behind her was Santa Barbara, nestled in the southern slopes of the Santa Ynez mountains. Santa Barbara: population, 74,400; mean summer temperature, seventy degrees; principal source of revenue, tourism. She smiled to herself. She couldn't help thinking like a marketing surveyor. That was good. Business was the reason she was here, supposedly, and the distracting tides of her personal life would not interfere with her job.

She wrapped her pink terry-cloth robe loosely around her and stepped out onto the balcony. Leaning against the damp wooden railing, she filled her lungs with the salty tang of the sea. She knew Derek wanted her to feel guilty, damn him. Today's painful lunch with

him shouldn't have been as difficult as it had turned out
to be, but he'd managed to make her out to be completely heartless. How naive of her to hope he would
understand and let her go out of his life easily. And
what a blessed relief it had been to have the perfect excuse for ending the no-win debate: "I have to get to
Santa Barbara," she'd insisted, then stood up and left
the little restaurant.

Within minutes her snappy white Mustang had been
whizzing along the coast highway heading north from
Los Angeles, racing away from the emotional blackmail that Derek was trying to trap her with. The top
was down and Leslie's shoulder-length black hair was
doing its best to wrench free from her Gucci scarf—a
gift from Derek.

The bracing September air had made her face tingle,
relaxing the tension lines that had grown so pro-
nounced on her forehead recently. Now, the week after
Labor Day, the beach towns were being recaptured by
the natives after the ritual frenzy of summer. Santa
Monica, Zuma, Malibu and all the favorite sun and surf
spots in between were returning to normal.

Summer had ended with a burst of heat, and the
temperature was settling down into the mid-seventies
along the Pacific shore. She had been impatient to get
away from Los Angeles and all it represented. After
three years of working as a willing slave for Olson and
Loeb, a large opinion-research firm, she had dared to
ask her boss, Justin Reiner, for an out-of-town assignment.

And dear Justin, asking no questions, had said, "Sure. I can send you up to Santa Barbara on Tuesday. We need a field survey there and you'll do fine. Mind you, it's not going to be easy in all that clean air and elegant Spanish atmosphere," he had warned with a wink. "But I've got a good new survey team ready, and you're just the one to direct it for me."

So here she was in glorious Santa Barbara, armed with a heavy notebook of statistics and field survey questions, ready to do a first-rate job for Justin. Her stomach tightened suddenly as her mind returned to the vexing problem of Derek and his stubborn pursuit of her. Where was his pride?

It had probably been a mistake to take Derek to Seattle last month to meet her family. She should have known how her mother would react, how delighted she would be to see what a presentable and bright young man Leslie was dating. Now she had pressure from two fronts, what with Derek and his ridiculous timetable for marriage.

"We'll be engaged by September and married before New Year's," he had told her mother confidently. "I'm an old-fashioned kind of guy."

And there Leslie had stood, tongue-tied, afraid that her very conservative parents would be shocked if she admitted her relationship with Derek was more an affair than a courtship. She was a long way from making a final commitment, no matter what Derek said.

In fact, she could have kicked herself for falling so easily into his experienced arms. She was mature enough at twenty-six not to be swept away by superficial masculine charm. There were other six-footers with dark wavy hair and penetrating eyes making the rounds of the unmarried women of Southern California. Derek wasn't unique in his far-reaching career goals, or even in his intellectual capacities. There were many times when she had to bite her tongue to avoid meeting one of his opinions head-on and setting him straight with her own.

She'd been lonely when he'd come into her life. Newly arrived from Seattle and still a bit unsure of herself in a big, impersonal city like Los Angeles, she had welcomed his enveloping attentions. It was a long time before she could admit to herself that she had, in a way, used Derek.

When he'd first said he loved her she'd wanted to believe him. Love was something she wanted very much, and he was good at making her feel like the most special woman in the world. Yet when they made love... Well, it was childish of her to be disappointed just because he didn't make bells ring for her.

She was beginning to think that his timetable might work, until one night last week when she had awakened in a cold sweat, trembling from a vague, threatening feeling that washed over her. At that moment, and without question, she knew she had to break away from the cocksure, overwhelming, railroad locomotive named Derek Parsons, Esq.

As for marriage—to anybody at all—she was in no hurry. She was happy with her budding marketing career. No longer a stranger to Los Angeles, she was eager to get on with her life in her own way, on her own terms—not as a satellite to anybody else.

She shrugged her robe closer around her and went back inside. One thing was certain: there wouldn't be any more phone calls from Derek. A call to the motel desk would take care of that.

"I'll be checking out in the morning," she informed the receptionist. "Can you have my bill ready by eight? And I don't want to accept any more phone calls, please."

Santa Barbara was full of other places she could stay. In her initial drive around town she had noticed how many turn-of-the-century houses had been converted to charming inns; they couldn't be more expensive than the chain motel she was staying in now. And she certainly didn't need the whirlpool tubs, the saunas and the nightclub. Besides, Justin Reiner wouldn't want the company to end up with a second-rate survey of the Santa Barbara area just because he'd given the job to a woman who didn't get enough sleep to do it right.

The thought that she could put herself beyond Derek's reach temporarily had a soothing effect on her nerves. She picked up the phone again, got an outside line and dialed Justin's home number, confident that at this hour he would be sipping a glass of his favorite brandy and listening to some obscure classical work on his stereo. He was a colorful character in the firm, absolutely tops in his profession. And he was very predictable. If she waited until morning to call him, he would already be jogging on San Vicente Boulevard, or out somewhere training new survey people.

"Hello, yes?" he answered in well-educated tones.

"Justin, it's Leslie. Sorry to call so late. What did I interrupt?"

"A lovely Vivaldi concerto. What's the problem, Leslie? Lonely for the office already?"

"Just wanted to clear something with you. I'm planning to check out of the motel in the morning and find a...uh...quieter place. I didn't want you trying to call here and finding I was gone." She could picture his blue-gray eyes crinkling with a smile, his sixty-year-old face looking like a leprechaun's.

"I'm glad I'm not young anymore," he responded sagely. "That was a song Maurice Chevalier sang, remember? Do whatever makes you comfortable, Leslie, but if I read your tone of voice correctly, this quieter place idea came up rather suddenly."

"I just don't want to mix my personal life up with my work. Do me a huge favor and don't tell anyone else where I'll be staying, please?"

"My pleasure. Do you know where you'll be?"

"As soon as I find myself a place, I'll call you. And thanks."

"For what?"

"For being a nice old coot who doesn't ask too many questions."

He gave a rumbling chuckle. "I don't need to. I've had all the romance I need, and I'm utterly content to leave it to the next generation now. You'll see. One of these days you'll wake up and wonder what all the fuss and thunder was about and Vivaldi will start looking awfully appealing as a nighttime companion."

"I'm not that cynical yet, Justin, but thanks for the jaded advice."

Another chuckle. "Have yourself a delightful stay wherever you end up. Good night, Leslie."

GREG AUSTIN sat brooding in the semidarkness of his office study, his tall muscular frame uncharacteristically slumped in the worn leather desk chair. He was obsessively turning one thought over and over in his mind, as he'd been doing all evening. Abruptly he swiveled the chair to an upright position and reached across the cluttered desk to pour another shot of bourbon into his glass. That was uncharacteristic, too. He swore softly when several amber drops stained one of his new field maps. A light knock at the door and the sound of Ofelia's voice brought him out of his reverie.

"I'm going now, Señor Austin," she said. "Davy's asleep and his lunch is packed in the refrigerator. I will be back tomorrow in time to meet him after school. Is there anything you need before I go?"

"Thanks, Ofelia, nothing. Give my best to your father." He heard the front door click shut. He should have been more sympathetic about the old man's illness. But then, he should have been a lot of things he wasn't. A rich man, for one. Then nobody would be trying to take his son from him.

But he wasn't rich; he wasn't even close. He was just a dirt geologist who taught his students at city college about the Earth, and he'd rather do that than be sitting snugly behind some desk at a big oil company. "Damned right," he growled aloud, and put his feet up on the desk in a gesture of defiance. He loved his work, he loved this old house he'd restored single-handedly, and he loved his son.

"That makes you an ornery son of a bitch, doesn't it?" he said into the darkness. He smiled grimly at the prospect of fighting for custody of Davy. But what if the fact that a child had a father who loved him had no bearing on the case? What if having wealthy grandparents made all the difference in a judge's decision?

For the thousandth time, he cursed himself for marrying Celeste Hartshorn. For the thousandth time, he stopped himself; if he hadn't married her he wouldn't have Davy.

He set down the glass and pushed away the court order that was the cause of his black mood. How could he explain to Davy that three weeks from now he might be living in Philadelphia with grandparents he hardly knew?

It was difficult to think about anything else right now, but he had to get his thoughts together for school tomorrow. Three classes of geology students were expecting Dr. Austin to talk about the history of the Earth, not the history of a failed marriage and a custody battle.

He strolled outside to clear his head and shake off the atmosphere of his office. Leaning against the railing of his spacious front porch, he inhaled the good Santa Barbara air and gazed into the distance where countless pinpoints of light sparkled from the far-off oil platforms.

Money and power weren't the only things that made the world go around, he reminded himself, then walked slowly back inside as the old grandfather clock in the hall struck midnight.

AT EIGHT O'CLOCK the next morning, Leslie stood at the checkout desk. "Were there any calls?" she asked as she paid her bill.

"No phone messages," replied the young assistant manager, "but a package was just brought in by a courier service. I was about to ring your room." He took a small square parcel from beneath the desk and gave it to her.

She didn't need to be psychic to know the package was from Derek. "Thanks," she said, dropping it quickly into her purse. What could he possibly have dreamed up since midnight? Part of her didn't want to know.

"Was anything wrong with the service?" the chatty red-haired man behind the desk asked. "Or was it just a change of plans? My manager doesn't want to lose customers because of bad service. Your reservation was originally for ten nights."

She smiled back. "A change of plans. And the service was fine. Tell your manager there was nothing wrong." She was eager to get away from the real possibility that Derek might call the motel any minute to see if she'd received his little package.

"Have a nice day," the friendly voice called to her departing back.

It felt good to be driving away from the motel. She found a hole-in-the-wall natural foods café on Lower State Street where she could relax over a cup of herbal tea and thumb through her Santa Barbara guidebook. Meanwhile, the package remained unopened in her purse. The way she was feeling today made her want to search for accommodations that would be warm and cosy, someplace that would give her a sense of normalcy at least, a place where the pictures weren't bolted down and she didn't feel so wretchedly off balance. But she couldn't take too much time finding her perfect hideaway. She jotted down the numbers of three small inns that offered bed and breakfast and went to the corner gas station to start calling.

The first, Grove House, took only weekend guests, and the next was full. The last place, Seaview Inn, was on Anacapa Street and the phone rang there several times before a man answered. Yes, he said, he was open and, yes, he had a room.

"I'd like an ocean view, if possible," she said. "Or maybe a view of the mission. And I'll be staying until the twenty-fourth."

"Can you speak louder, please? You sound like you're in the middle of a highway."

Two refrigerated produce trucks were rumbling past on their way to the freeway. Leslie repeated her request in a loud voice.

"You'd have to come now, if you want the room. I can't wait any longer than fifteen minutes for you. I'm just out the door for the day."

"Right now is fine!" she shouted above the grinding gears of another truck. She started to ask him if her room had a private telephone, but the man had already hung up. His response was not her idea of a hearty country inn welcome. Bordering on curt, in fact, she thought peevishly.

She was feeling prickly about moody men, especially since lunch yesterday, and last night's midnight call.... She pressed one hand over her stomach, hoping that the heavy, dull ache would go away by itself. *No more guilt, please*, she silently prayed as she picked up her purse and briefcase and went to her car. She knew she had to open Derek's package before she began her business day—open it, work through the feelings connected with it and get on with her responsibilities. She couldn't have him dogging her emotions this way.

Sitting in her car with the top down and the crisp morning sea air whipping the ends of her straight dark hair around her face, Leslie drew a deep breath and tore the gold paper wrapping from the little box.

A small sheet of Derek's elegant parchment notepaper was tied into a scroll that lay diagonally on a bed of jeweler's cotton. She gingerly slipped off the silver cord, allowing the crisp, expensive paper to spring open and reveal a second paper object rolled inside it.

Beneath the embossed monogram of his stationery he had penned one word: "Remember!"

It took a long moment for Leslie to connect the message with the second object—a round cocktail coaster—but when she did her heart lurched. The Hotel del Coronado. How clever of him to choose that particular memento to send her, now that she was alone in another seaside resort.

She hurried to stuff the disturbing item into the glove compartment, to remove it from her sight. Of course he knew she would remember. How could she forget?

They had been in one of the Coronado's expensive guest suites on a warm night in early June. "I love you, Leslie," he had whispered to her as he'd carried her over the threshold of their airy, beautiful room. They were the right words after the weeks of sensual tension that had been building between them. She had tried so hard to keep their relationship light, but finally her resistance had crumbled. She blamed her weakness on the power of the moon, the stars, the lapping waves of a summer ocean, the little dance band in the Coronado's open air summer dining room...and then the long walk hand in hand to the suite in a very private corner of the romantic old hotel.

"No regrets?" he had asked her as he nuzzled the hair away from her cheek sometime in the middle of their long night together.

And what had she answered? It didn't matter now. She hadn't said she loved him, she knew that. She'd thought of it as an affair from the very first night—exciting, glamorous, but not forever. Derek was the kind of complimentary, bring-you-a-gift, remember-your-cat's-birthday kind of man women wrote novels about. Yet something inside her always knew it would have to end.

She cut herself off in midthought and turned her key in the ignition. Checking the city map on the seat beside her she started driving north on Anacapa Street. A few blocks up she passed Grove House and wished she were staying there; homey with a shady forest of dark green avocado trees almost hiding the inviting low bungalow, it radiated peace. Leslie sighed as she drove on toward the hills behind the central part of town.

There, the streets were shaded by very old trees, towering eucalyptus and sycamores, and the houses all seemed to have large windows facing the sea, as if the ocean was a kind of blue Mecca.

Crossing Padre Street onto Anacapa, Leslie found what she was looking for. A neat wooden sign painted in the same cream and blue colors as the tall, turreted Victorian house behind it said Seaview Inn. She turned in to the gravel driveway and crunched to a stop.

Someone had done a masterful job of restoring the old house with its lacy woodwork along the upstairs balconies and the little white gazebo just visible in the side flower garden among masses of blooming roses. A riot of red and purple geraniums tumbled from painted wood planters along the broad front porch. Leslie sat for a moment, lost in admiration. This lovely haven was a very pleasant surprise after that abrupt telephone conversation.

An aura of removal from everyday cares shimmered all around the complicated outlines of the house. With her anticipation reviving, Leslie lifted her luggage from the back seat and walked up the twelve white steps to the front door, where a cut-glass peep window was covered inside by a dainty ecru-colored lace curtain.

The polished brass plate next to the door read, Please Ring Bell. She gave a firm pull to the brass chain next to the plaque, half expecting a character from *Alice in Wonderland* to hurry past her. The place was perfect, just perfect for her hideaway.

Looking around her from the immaculate porch she could see the craggy Channel Islands making an effort to jut up from the low fog banks that engulfed them. At the sound of heavy footsteps approaching, she turned back to face the house. The door opened swiftly with a whoosh and a very tall man who filled the entrance-way with his imposing figure looked down at her. "Oh, it's you," he said. "I was expecting the plumber."

She pulled back a little. "If it's not convenient—"

"No . . . forgive me," he interrupted in a more courteous tone. "It's just that a pipe decided to burst in the laundry room, and I'm late for a class, and my house-keeper is out for most of the day."

"Really, if it's a problem I can come back later." She was already mentally going down the list of possible alternative accommodations.

"No, don't." He reached for her luggage and started inside. "I can't afford to alienate a guest. I don't suppose you know much about plumbing?"

"Not a thing." Just then she noticed his agate-green eyes. She also noticed his deep tan, the strong hands and the wet khaki work shirt that clung to his broad, well-muscled chest. California rugged, her analytical mind said, while her senses jumped with pleasure.

"Well, my hundred-year-old water line is starting to give up, and I can't let it do that, not right now. Listen, Miss . . ."

"O'Neill."

"Why don't I take your things upstairs, and you can check in formally later on. I'm not the genial host right now. When Ofelia shows up, she'll take care of signing you in."

Leslie followed him up the straight, steep staircase, taking in the walls hung with old framed photographs of early Santa Barbara. The light wood floors were polished to a high natural gloss, and the upstairs landing revealed a broad hallway decorated with intricate plaster scrollwork patterns. Streaks of amber light filtered down from a stained glass skylight overhead.

"Here it is, miss. The room with the ocean view." He opened the door wide, set down her bags and turned to leave. "Sorry about everything," he said distractedly. "You'll like Ofelia."

"Thanks." She watched him run down the stairs, two at a time. Turning back into her room, she discovered herself in a time capsule of sorts. A lace-covered canopy bed with an antique patchwork quilt, a marble-topped oak table with a pink flowered pitcher and washbowl, a bright braided rug next to the bed, a dark rocking chair with a needlepoint cushion of roses and an oak armoire that almost brushed the ceiling all contributed to her first impression. She went to the large front window, pulled back the lace curtains and opened the casement. The view was equally charming.

Outside, the proprietor's old Jeep was just coming around from the rear of the property. Leslie watched as it screeched to a sudden stop in front of the house. Honking the horn, the man leaned out, looking up at her. "Miss . . . could I ask a favor?" he called up. "If the plumber comes before you go out again, tell him I couldn't wait for him. But don't let him leave without fixing the mess in the laundry room." He drove off with a crunch of gravel, while Leslie smiled to herself. *Well, you wanted homey, and you don't get much homier than this. . . .*

2

LESLIE UNPACKED, hanging her clothes in the cavernous armoire and laying out her personal items on the huge white pedestal sink in the en-suite bathroom. She was looking forward to her first bath in the claw-footed enamel tub. The antique standing mirror in the corner was dappled with age. Even the toilet was a relic of times gone by. She pulled the handle on the long chain, causing a rush of water to drop suddenly from the high cabinet overhead into the bowl. A shuddering groan rattled the pipes afterward. The bathroom was going to be fun, she decided happily.

Justin had arranged a ten-thirty meeting of her survey team in a conference room at the city college. Even though she was a veteran of sorts with Olson and Loeb, this was her first assignment as a team leader and she wanted to look as if she knew what she was doing. She piled her hair into a loose swirl at the back of her head, her usual business look. With her glowing tan, the result of a long summer of weekend outings, she needed no makeup except for a hint of mauve liner to bring out the deep flecks of hidden color in her warm brown eyes.

Several years ago she had discovered the Los Angeles garment district with its stark showrooms of cut-rate designer clothes. The dress she wore now was well cut to show off her high, firm breasts and small waist; it represented one of her latest victories in the crowded dressing rooms of the Cooper Building. Derek had admired her good taste, but he'd never approved of her shopping on Santee, San Julian and Los Angeles streets. On the other hand, Leslie was equally uncomfortable with his sometimes conspicuous spending in the more fashionable streets of Los Angeles.

Picking up her purse, briefcase and microcassette recorder, she prepared to leave. Now, was she supposed to have her own key to the house? Or to her room? Bed and breakfast protocol was obviously not the same as a traditional hotel's. That was already clear.

A quick exploration of her room revealed a large white envelope inscribed To Our Guests. Inside were two keys attached to a heavy brass ring, one for the front door and one for the room. There was a booklet of things to do and places to visit in the Santa Barbara area and a single typed sheet of house rules.

If she understood correctly, she could expect a bountiful breakfast in the morning, an optional boxed lunch prepared by the housekeeper and a complimentary glass of sherry set by her bed each evening. "You are part of our family," it read, "and we will try to answer every need you have. Just ask. The Seaview Inn wants to become a tradition with you, as it is to so many other guests whom we consider to be our dear friends." It was signed "Greg Austin, Prop."

Well, that was much better. Not quite the haphazard management it had first appeared to be.

She went downstairs, this time noticing the comfortable parlor and dining room, the old brass ceiling fixtures and wall sconces that still had knobs for regulating the gas, even though they had been converted to electricity. Apparently, she was alone in the house. As she was stepping out the door, a telephone rang. She hesitated, then decided to answer it.

The sound was coming from behind a closed door off the parlor. Leslie picked up the phone on the fourth ring, diving over piles of maps on the big desk to reach it in time.

"Who is this, please?" the woman's voice asked.

"A guest at the inn. May I take a message?"

"Señor Austin is not there? I wish to speak with him."

"He left a few minutes ago."

"Oh, I forget, he has his school starting today. But I have a big problem." The Spanish-accented voice sounded close to breaking.

Leslie's natural instincts were to get involved, even though she hadn't a minute to spare if she was to be on time for her meeting. "Is there anything I can do?"

"My father is very sick and I cannot leave him today. Tell Señor Austin that Ofelia is sorry, she won't be coming back to the inn this afternoon. I will call him in the morning."

"I'll tell him."

"Oh, and the most important thing. I cannot meet Davy at the bus stop."

"Who?"

"His little boy, coming home from school at two o'clock. Maybe you can meet him, Miss..."

"O'Neill, Leslie O'Neill. Let me get this straight. There's a child who expects to be met at a bus stop—"

"*Sí*, at the corner where the big white house has the oak tree that is on the ground. You'll see it."

"Listen, ma'am . . . Ofelia . . . I'm not sure I can do it. I'm just going out. I'll leave a message for Mr. Austin. Maybe he'll be back before then."

"He never come back before three. I can't talk longer. Davy is the one with the red hair and the yellow tennis shoes. *Adiós, y muchas gracias.*"

Leslie stood staring at the phone in her hand. Then she searched the messy desk for a clean sheet of paper and a pen. While she was writing down Ofelia's message, the phone rang again.

What now? "Hello?"

"Mrs. Austin? Jack the plumber. I can't get a man out there until later today. How bad is the leak?"

"The laundry room's flooded, and Mr. Austin should be home around three."

"Well, it can't climb the cellar stairs before then," he replied with a chuckle. "About time you gave up on those old lines into the house, don't you think . . . bring it all up to code?"

"Yes . . . well, thanks for calling, Jack. I'll leave a note for Mr. Austin."

"I'll be there sometime before five, I expect. And tell that man of yours he's a lucky son of a gun to have teachers' hours instead of a plumber's." He gave a good-natured laugh.

Leslie kept the phone off the hook until she had finished her revised note. She found a roll of clear tape in the top desk drawer, then dashed to the front door, leaving the note taped just above the scrollwork on the knob. She hurried to her car, determined that the phone wouldn't ring until she was out of earshot.

It was nearly ten-thirty; she hated being late for appointments. Fortunately, she had imprinted the route to the college on her memory earlier this morning, a talent she'd developed during her part-time college job as a courier.

The shortest way to the campus took her through neighborhoods of run-down houses where most of the residents appeared to be of Latin descent. Even in her rush she noted the location of a tortilla factory, where she intended to return later. Freshly made corn tortillas were a rare treat for a city girl whose apartment was set right in the middle of a Hollywood fast-foods ghetto. The *tortillería* sent its delicious aromas out for a block in every direction.

She screeched around the final corner and into the parking lot of the administration building. Hoping that her four ladies and two men wouldn't see, she actually ran the last hundred feet to the meeting room.

Bless you, Justin, she thought half an hour later as she sat amid the comfortable friendliness of her well-trained and eager survey team. With their chairs arranged in a circle, they were discussing hypothetical situations and having a good time doing it. Justin's field schedule called for one day of orientation, seven days of survey work and two days when Leslie would evaluate the project and do last-minute spot checks at the survey sites.

Essentially, the survey consisted of showing a person several types of magazine ads, from sophisticated and understated to blatant and gaudy. The questionnaire was designed to show the degree of pleasure, attraction or just plain irritation that the ad evoked. Justin was aiming for a large cross section of respondents in order to provide an accurate sampling of the market for several national advertising campaigns.

"First the opinion survey, then everything falls into place—brainstorming sessions, artwork, clever jingles. But without first knowing the public's tastes, you're just pouring good advertising money down the rat hole." Justin had said that so many times that Leslie imagined it was probably tattooed across his chest.

She divided her people into three groups, which she would monitor on a rotating basis. Two students would be canvassing several colleges in the area; a husband-and-wife team, newly retired from their own mail-order business, would spend the week at the largest mall in town; and two housewives, who were only working mornings, would be posted outside the major supermarkets.

They all had lunch together in the student center, talking until everyone felt secure enough to begin the job. Leslie gave each of them the number of the inn in case of emergencies. She planned to do some interviewing on the campus herself in the afternoon, but she kept thinking about a little red-haired boy standing alone at his bus stop.

It was nearly two o'clock when she parked her car at the corner of Anacapa and Padre Streets, in front of a white house that had a fallen oak tree in its yard. Three children stepped from the school bus; one had a shock of red hair that couldn't be missed.

"Davy?" she called out the window.

The boy stopped, but kept his distance.

"I'm a guest at the inn. My name's Leslie. Ofelia called to ask me to meet you and take you home. Is that all right with you?" She could see that he wasn't sure he should be talking to strangers.

"I'm okay," he said firmly and started walking down the street.

"Do you have a key?"

"My dad's gonna let me in." His jaw jutted stubbornly.

Leslie knew she had worried the boy, but she couldn't have him locked out of the house. She started the car again and drove around the block, arriving ahead of him to open the front door. When he saw her inside with a key in her hand he seemed to realize that she wasn't a kidnapper. "I'm sorry to frighten you, Davy," she said, extending her hand to his. "But your dad's still at school and Ofelia couldn't leave her sick father."

Familiar agate-green eyes studied her from a height of three feet. "I wasn't scared. I just like to walk fast, that's all."

Leslie followed his thin energetic body into the kitchen and watched him search the refrigerator for food. "Ofelia always has stuff for me," he said hopefully.

"If you don't mind being with me for an hour or two, I can buy you something refreshing at the city college. I have some work to do there."

"Are you gonna work with my dad?"

"Is that where he is? The college?"

"He teaches big kids about rocks and stuff. I got to watch him once."

"Then let's go!" It would be simple to locate Greg Austin and deliver Davy to him, then she could get on with her job.

LESLIE PEERED into the geology lecture room through the window in the door. Class was just breaking up. Greg Austin was surrounded by students, a large percentage of them female, as he handed out stapled sheafs of class notes. He had the kind of looks that belonged in a Western clothing commercial—small hips, long legs, broad chest and an apparently careless but unmistakably masculine style of dressing. Leslie was pretty sure he didn't notice the way his female students looked at him. More of the unobservant man's man type, she thought, not unappreciatively.

"Do you want to see your dad?" she said, lifting Davy up to the window. He weighed about as much as her office typewriter.

A moment later Greg Austin was at the door with his son in his arms. "How come?" he demanded. "Where's Ofelia?"

"Her father's ill. She couldn't meet your son, so I did."

"And what did Davy do?" he asked with a stern eye toward the boy.

"He behaved like any well-trained child. He wouldn't have anything to do with a stranger. I let him walk home alone and then met him at the front door."

"Good boy," he praised, swinging Davy around and down again. "Thanks, Miss..."

"O'Neill. No problem. I was coming back here, anyway, on business. Glad I could help. I'll see you later, then?"

He put a detaining hand out to touch her shoulder. "What about Ofelia?"

"I left you a long note on the front door. She isn't coming back tonight, but she'll call in the morning. I hope you don't mind, but I went into your study to answer the phone."

"Not a bit. Miss...O'Neill." He smiled. "How would you like to have dinner with two hungry bachelors tonight?"

"Two?" she repeated curiously.

"Davy and me. I cook good camp food, that's all. Without Ofelia we'd starve. How about it?"

Suddenly, it was all Leslie could do not to reach up and brush his heavy fall of dark blond hair back from his forehead. His smile was completely... well...nice, incapable of concealing motives or of being used deviously. What a beautiful smile, she mused. She had never before seen an adult face that conveyed such disarming openness.

"I'd love to keep you both company. I have a couple of hours' more work here and then I'm free." She tried not to stare at Greg Austin's dappled green eyes. This morning he had been no more than a blur to her senses, but now she realized he was definitely a compelling male specimen.

"Downstairs at six okay?" he asked, putting a loving hand on Davy's tousled head. "Nothing fancy."

Leslie waved her agreement and walked back to the student center where she spent the rest of her workday interviewing. Her entire survey experience had been in the big city arena of Los Angeles, and she was pleasantly surprised to find a far more friendly and cooperative reception on this bustling small-town campus. Justin had always told her that New York, Chicago and Los Angeles were the toughest opinion areas of all, but she had thought he was just trying to build up her confidence. Along the way these past two years, she had also acquired the ability to handle most situations. As she got into her car and drove away from the pretty, eucalyptus-shaded campus overlooking the marina, she found herself using one of Justin's pet phrases. Santa Barbara did look as if it would be "a piece of cake," just as he'd promised.

HER GIANT, CLAW-FOOTED BATHTUB was a challenge to approach, requiring a hefty step up just to get into it. But the effort was worth it. Lying there letting the tension created by Derek, a new assignment and everything else flow out of her, she stared at the decorated ceiling overhead. Floral garlands swagged around the perimeter in raised plaster, a pleasing soft blue against the eggshell background color. Outside the two narrow arched bathroom windows she saw the gently waving branches of a sycamore tree, its leaves starting to turn with early autumn colors.

Rather nice, she breathed peacefully to herself, feeling satisfied that she had called Justin, met her team, done some sampling and didn't have to wonder where she'd be having dinner tonight.

There were still no signs of other guests, or anybody else for that matter, not even the noises that a little boy would make. Yet the house didn't seem so large that two other people would be able to disappear into it completely.

Dumb curiosity, she scolded and turned her mind to finding something to wear tonight. Her lavender silk jump suit with the long pink sash would do—not too dressy—and flat sandals.

Without having gone to the best private schools and learned the subtle mannerisms that bespoke class, Leslie still carried herself with innate elegance. Her mother said it came from her grandmother, who had also endowed her with those high cheekbones, the straight, thick ebony crown of hair, and the forthright honesty that sometimes bordered on bluntness.

She brushed out her hair, letting it hang loose so it just grazed her shoulders, then went down the steep stairs to the parlor where a cheery fire crackled and period furniture filled the comfortable, inviting room. The broad bow window had a curved and cushioned window seat. Leslie perched there while she absorbed the architectural touches that made the house so delightful.

A glass-fronted bookcase stood next to the carved wooden mantelpiece. Leslie walked over to it, half expecting to find nineteenth-century authors represented in the little collection. Instead she found books by the Western writer Brett Harte, modern field guides to birds and California mountain trails, a book about restoring Victorian-era houses and a number of popular paperbacks that would make easy bedtime reading. What interested her most, however, was the old family Bible that lay on its side on the top shelf, its worn leather heavily embossed with gold Gothic lettering. Her mother had a Bible like this one; it had been passed on through four generations.

She opened one cabinet door to get a closer look at the huge book. Lifting the heavy cover, she read the inscription on the flyleaf: Jeremiah Justin, 1868. It hadn't been dusted for a long time, which tempted Leslie to lift it out and blow gently across the top. But as she did, a photograph slipped out from between the pages and dropped onto the floor.

With the book balanced in one arm she bent to pick up the picture. It was a modern family grouping—a very handsome and youthful Greg Austin, well dressed and smiling was posed next to a stunning young dark-haired woman and an infant.

"That's Davy and me in another life." Her host's voice came from behind her. When she turned around, his face belied the casual comment.

"I didn't mean to intrude," she said, starting to return the book to the shelf.

"It doesn't much matter, anyway," he replied cryptically.

Leslie felt uncomfortable and regretted having stumbled on the photograph. "I'm not normally a busybody," she said, trying to establish a better mood in the quickly thickening atmosphere of the parlor. "I was really just dusting off your beautiful old Bible."

"Well, dust to dust, they say. Right?" He smiled, but it wasn't one of the smiles she had enjoyed that afternoon.

"Now if Davy ever finishes tying his shoes, we can get some food. He's still dawdling up in the tower." He quickly left the room again through a far door behind the parlor.

Leslie heard him climbing a flight of back stairs and realized that the high, decorative turret on the house was probably the family's private quarters. *The tower,* she repeated to herself.

The two Austin men returned in a moment, ready to go out. Greg gave Leslie a hand up into the Jeep and Davy scrambled into the back seat. "Just shove some of the mess out of your way," she was told. "This is my office as well as my horse."

Arranging her feet around an old, dented metal toolbox, she tried not to think about what sort of dust and grime her lavender silk was encountering. With amusement she caught herself noticing that nobody had complimented her on looking terrific. In fact, nobody seemed to care how she looked. What vanity she had developed in the past six months with Derek. It was almost a relief to be treated like one of the family instead of a china doll.

Greg attempted to make small talk, then fell silent in the wake of Davy's nonstop chatter. The boy continued to dominate the conversation all the way to the sawdust-on-the-floor family restaurant in a large shopping plaza north of town, which was just as well. After they had ordered their assorted hamburgers, salad for Leslie, and iced drinks, Greg stayed inside his personal dark cloud. He let Davy do most of the talking for both of them. The atmosphere was strained. Finally, he brought out his wallet, dropped a ten-dollar bill and some change on the table, and stood up. "Bedtime. School tomorrow, kiddo."

Davy obediently gulped the last of his cola drink and stuffed the rest of his hamburger into his mouth. They all returned to the car, Leslie anxious to get back to the privacy of her room.

Dinner had been an uncomfortable experience at best. Whatever had set Greg Austin off was beyond her, and she didn't even want to know what it was. At least Davy was a companionable type. *Deliver me from moody men*, she thought darkly as they entered the rear door of the inn.

Davy said good-night and ran upstairs, while Greg thanked Leslie again for picking up his son. She couldn't resist saying, "You really shouldn't let him eat all that junk. The additives alone are enough to mutate his genes." The words were out before she realized that she was using them to vent her frustration with things in general, and not Greg Austin in particular.

Instead of firing a remark back at her, he started to laugh, the sound erupting from deep within his chest. "That's great!" he managed to say, "Ofelia must have sent you to badger me!"

Seeing that he was genuinely cheerful again, she ventured a smile. "Well, you weren't exactly attentive to his health tonight. I would think that a man who understands the Earth and its gifts would want his son to know about them, too . . . if I'm not intruding again where I'm not invited."

"Oh, no. You're not." His ruddy face was kind now. "I don't mind a tongue-lashing now and again." He reached out a hand to take hers. "Thanks for bringing me back down with a thud. It's been a crazy time for me lately. You've probably decided I'm completely uncivilized." His smile was there again, like a beckoning hearth fire. His whole face radiated a life force that made her think of untamed wilderness.

"Things have been a little crazy for me, too," she admitted as she took his hand; it enclosed hers with a strong, warm grip. She didn't want to let go. Something wonderful was contained in the small space between their two hands—not exactly sensuality, not possession—just something very wonderful. She pulled her eyes away, breaking what must have seemed to be her ridiculous concentration on their hands. "Well," she whispered awkwardly, "I've got to get some sleep. Thanks for dinner."

Greg relaxed his grip on her hand, aware that he shouldn't be feeling anything like what he was feeling—not now. His life was about as upside down as it could possibly be these days. He mumbled something about seeing her in the morning, about Ofelia coming back to fix a healthy breakfast and not worrying about registering tonight—trying to sound casual. Casual didn't come easily while his heart was pounding this way.

He thought about reminding her that she had a complimentary glass of sherry coming to her. Instead, he said good-night, put one foot ahead of the other on the curving staircase of the tower and closed the heavy door of his large Spartan bedroom behind him.

3

A LIGHT TAP on her bedroom door pulled Leslie up from sleep. "Here's your orange juice" came Davy's chirping voice.

Leslie smiled. "Thanks. I'll be up in a minute to get it."

"My dad says to come 'n' eat." The departing footsteps thudded away from the door and down the stairs.

Leslie opened her eyes to her sun-filled room. The yellow daisy-patterned wallpaper made her feel like a little girl again instead of the restless woman she was. Restless mostly because she could feel Derek's frustration reaching out toward her, and she still felt a pang of guilt about his reaction to the breakup. He had insisted that he loved her, but what did that really mean?

Derek will get over it, maybe faster than you think, she told herself as she pulled aside her soft comforter and stepped from bed. Marriage to Derek wouldn't have left room for Leslie O'Neill, the intelligent woman who had a degree in business from the University of Oregon and was having a wonderful time learning marketing research from the bottom up. Now if she could just use these precious ten days on Justin's assignment and get her feet planted firmly back on the ground . . .

It was after seven o'clock when she finished dressing for the long working day ahead. Downstairs she expected to find the elusive Ofelia in charge of those delicious smells that were wafting through the house. Instead, she was met in the airy kitchen by Davy and his father.

Greg looked up from his chores. "Eat at your own risk. Ofelia isn't coming back until noon."

He scooped a serving of eggs onto a plate and set it on the round wooden table in the center of the room. "Nothing poisonous, I promise." He grinned and held out one of the wooden ladder-back chairs for her. Like a good host he eased her chair into place, leaning close for a moment.

Leslie's nerves reacted to the subtle electricity of his body so near hers. It was a pleasurable sensation; he reminded her of sunlight and sweet earth. Even after he turned away she felt a tingling awareness of him.

"Did you sleep well?" he asked.

Did she? With all the jangling thoughts competing inside her head for attention she was lucky to have slept at all. "If I didn't, it wasn't the fault of my beautiful room. Really, you've done a fantastic job. Did some of the antique furniture come from your family or did you have to collect every piece separately?"

"I'm something of a natural scout. Weekends spent at swap meets and estate sales, a little bartering for my geological services . . . that kind of thing. The old grandfather clock in the hall was payment for my discovering well water under a man's property. Water's in short supply around here. I think the clock was his prized possession, he was so grateful."

"And you did the restoration yourself?"

"As much as I could, with as little interference from the powers that be as I could get away with. I'm kind of a maverick that way."

"But the decorating—all the little touches that make the inn feel so much a part of the last century. You did all that, too?" She looked around at the highly polished copper pots that hung from antique iron hooks above the tiled sink. The curtains at the windows were fresh and crisp, repeating the traditional colors of the Mexican tiles.

"Ofelia handled the kitchen," he said, gesturing with his spatula as he hovered over the sizzling pancakes on the large griddle. "And I have some friends who're very good at decorating. I had a little help along the way." Female help, of course. What normal woman would refuse that appealing smile and his special brand of rough charm?

She found herself staring at his broad back while he flipped the golden pancakes onto a Mexican-style serving plate. "I thought you couldn't cook. More modesty?" His faded blue Western shirt and worn jeans looked as if they had been designed with him in mind. She couldn't imagine him in a business suit.

He looked up. "I told you I did camp food. That's all this is. If you want anything more you've come to the wrong place. There's a Cordon Bleu chef at the Grove Inn—quiches served at the drop of a hat. But you'll pay French prices for them, too."

"I'm basically a pancake-and-eggs girl myself," Leslie assured him, then wondered why she had gone out of her way to tell him that half-truth. Hadn't she unabashedly reveled in her share of gourmet goodies and sworn that nouvelle cuisine was the closest thing to heaven?

He dropped two crisp bacon slices onto her dish next to the aromatic herbed eggs, then planted Davy in a chair and sat down himself. "I didn't think to ask last night—are you on vacation here in Santa Barbara?"

He hadn't thought to say much of anything last night. "I'm here on business. I work for an opinion-research company in Los Angeles."

The changeable green eyes across from her lost their warm light for an instant. "A career woman," he commented as he slathered butter on his pancakes.

"Trying to be," she said. "It's my first time on my own in a new territory." She didn't want to sound defensive, but he'd said "career woman" with such distaste it bothered her. She ate quietly for a while, checking her watch now and then, aware of her host's eyes still on her.

"If I can help by giving my opinion on anything, I'd be glad to," Greg offered.

"Opinions about women who work, or opinions about products?" she asked.

"Was I that obvious? Sorry. I have nothing against a woman pursuing whatever career she wants, as long as it doesn't hurt the people around her. Too many women just say adios to everything and—" He turned to see

Davy's interested young face. "Off with you, sport. Get your stuff for school. We're leaving in a minute."

Davy reluctantly left the table where he had been on his best behavior, intently watching his father talk with the new guest. Leslie patted her lips with her calico napkin. "Me too—I've got to meet two of my team at the mall." She was in a rush to leave the kitchen before Greg decided to finish his last sentence and tell her more than she wanted to hear about women who say adios to their men.

She could imagine what was in his past: a wife who took off to follow some personal career plans, someone who didn't pay enough attention to their child. Somewhere along the way Greg had ended up a single father with his own ideas about what women want out of life.

"Breakfast was terrific," she complimented as she left the table. "But I still haven't registered. Should I wait for Ofelia, or—"

"First night's free for you." Greg untied his cook's apron and lobbed it toward the sink. "I've treated you like a hired hand already, so I can't possibly charge you for last night." He stood up, reaching to hold the swinging door open for her. His height emphasized his handsomeness, that potent aura of male energy that crackled so close to the surface. "Anyway, you didn't even get your bedtime glass of sherry."

"I'll probably need it tonight. It's going to be a long day for me," she told him, not quite sure that the touch of intimacy in his statement was an intentional part of his offer. Best to assume that it wasn't. She kept walking toward the staircase, then looked back at him. "I can't let you give me a break on the lodging, really. My company expects a bill for each night. They might think I was taking a vacation, and it would only complicate their bookkeeping. But thanks, anyway. By the way, I need to use a telephone where there's a little privacy. Yesterday I made a call to my boss from a phone booth next to the student center at the college and couldn't hear a thing."

"Be my guest," he said. "There's a phone in the parlor. Just be sure to get time and charges from the operator." He stood looking down at her as if he hadn't decided whether to say something more to her. "I hope this comes out right, but I keep having the feeling we've met before."

Leslie shook her head. "I probably just look like someone. This is my first time in Santa Barbara."

"Philadelphia, maybe?"

"Not there, either. Sorry." She wished she could already be past him and safely inside the parlor. He wasn't the kind of man one could ignore, any more than one could avoid being aware of the clean natural scent of him. He didn't use cologne, she noted.

"I'm sorry, too," he said with a shrug, but his eyes stayed on her face, making a careful analysis of her features.

"Well, I . . ." she ventured into the awkward silence. "Maybe I'll call the office later. Thanks again for breakfast." She turned and went upstairs, but not as fast as she wanted. She wanted to run away from that unnerving fascination that consumed her whenever she was within ten feet of this man. He was such a perfect companion for his old house, exhilarating and down-to-earth, cut from a pattern that wasn't in fashion any more, but that still had a nostalgic appeal to the heart. It had to do with home and everything that home could mean to a woman. Yet there was more, she had to admit—much more than just hominess.

Back in her room she picked up her handbag, taking one last bemused look around her. It was a temptation to chuck everything and play hooky in this delightful hideaway. Obviously it wasn't good for her to fantasize too much here, imagining things she had no business thinking. But wouldn't it be sheer pleasure to lie back under the lace canopy while Greg Austin served her sherry in bed tonight!

From her window she saw Greg and Davy in the Jeep turning onto Anacapa Street. This was just another day for father and son, but so very strange for her. She shouldn't be remembering last night's touch of the hand with Greg, or the disturbing intensity of this morning's casual banter. To be noticing any man at all, this soon, was ridiculous. She had a momentary thought about poor Derek, but his face was a blur in her mind. She couldn't even bring up a clear picture of his eyes—were they brown or hazel? She knew very well the color of Greg Austin's eyes. Green, they were—like the hills he walked with those battered old boots of his—deep with overtones of summer changing to fall. They were eyes that she would have difficulty forgetting, no matter how much time went by.

GREG LEFT DAVY at school and drove down State Street to keep an early appointment with his lawyer. Jim Vargas, being his usual wry self this morning, told Greg that he wouldn't get to his office this early for anyone but an impoverished geologist who probably couldn't pay him half what he was worth for his legal advice.

"I must be crazy." Jim laughed. "I should be holding some rich widow's hand right now instead of crusading for truth and justice."

Greg and Jim had belonged to the same hiking club at university and their friendship was built on trust and mutual admiration. "Just tell me, Jim," Greg said, "what are the chances they'll take Davy from me? The court date's in three weeks."

"Take a deep breath, *compadre*," the dark-haired lawyer suggested. "I can't guarantee anything. I don't know the kind of judge you'll be facing. But generally the natural father gets priority in a custody case like this. Unless..."

"Unless what?" Greg prompted impatiently.

"Unless the grandparents can make it look like you aren't providing adequate care for Davy."

"Horse manure!" he exploded, adding an equally descriptive Spanish oath. "Let 'em try!"

Jim put up a hand. "I'm only telling you the worst that could happen. Lawyers are supposed to do that, you know. Frankly, I think that the fact you own the inn and have a housekeeper will be in your favor. Also, the fact that you're starting your own consulting business and have your job at the college makes you seem stable."

LESLIE GAVE HERSELF an hour alone in the Seaview Inn after Greg and Davy had left, just to collect herself. She wandered around the old house with a growing appreciation for the care taken in its restoration. On the parlor wall was a series of photographs dated 1983, showing the weathered gray structure as it had looked when Greg had bought it; unkempt garden and tangled vines hid most of the house, and the windows in the round corner tower were broken and the front porch sagged. She admired the drive and energy it must have taken to revive that derelict Victorian house and create the Seaview. She could imagine how Greg had felt in accepting such a challenge and then overcoming it. There was that kind of daring in her own blood, even though the world had yet to see it.

She was curious about the tower rooms. She wanted to see what kind of an environment Greg would create for his own use, but a respectful part of her nature kept her from peeking up the curved staircase. Privacy was important to her; she wouldn't violate someone else's. Instead she stayed in the parlor and called her office.

Justin Reiner's secretary, Marie, told her that Derek had been calling and urgently wanted to get in touch with her. "I told a little lie to him, Leslie," Marie said. "Justin said you didn't want anyone to have your number in Santa Barbara, so I said we didn't have it. I hated doing it, he sounded so upset. . . ."

"That's okay, Marie. I'll take care of it. Tell Justin I checked in and everything's going fine. And thanks for the white lie. It was important to me."

"*Seem* stable! What more do they want from me?"

"A wife, for one thing, and a comfortable bank account. But since you don't have either of those, you'll just have to charm the judge. That's the best I can advise. Oh, and leave your colorful temper outside the courtroom. I imagine the Philadelphia courts won't appreciate bilingual cursing or your brand of California informality."

Greg sat and ground his teeth while he tried to quell his irritation with Mr. and Mrs. Paul Hartshorn and all they represented—money, power and influence.

"I'll marry when I'm damned well ready, and I'm sure as hell not ready now!" He scowled back at Jim's slight look of amusement.

"Poor girl who gets you is all I can say. So determined to do things your way that you'd even argue over the best way to skin a rattlesnake while the varmint was still alive and shaking his tail at you."

"What's that supposed to mean? I'm too pigheaded for my own good?"

"Just cool it this one time, Greg, I beg you. Hold your fire in Philadelphia. Let everyone have his say, and then you have yours."

"I let everyone have his say three years ago, and that's why I got into this mess to begin with," he muttered.

"All the grandparents have is temporary custody, and you know why that happened."

"Sure. They were lying bastards who told some judge I had deserted my son. What a load of—"

"Shut up, amigo," Jim said quietly. "You were the one who was so mad at his wife's social life that he took a harebrained job for six months mapping wilderness trails in some godforsaken part of the northern Rockies. What were the Hartshorns supposed to do when their daughter suddenly died and nobody could find you?"

"Whose side are you on, anyway?" Greg barked. "The forest service knew damned well how to locate me. Paul Hartshorn just wanted to keep me out of the picture so he could snatch Davy. I had every right to take him back and come out here to California."

Jim looked down at the thick file in front of him and read aloud. "'The natural father then proceeded to abduct the boy and remove him from the legal custody of his grandparents.'"

"Hell, Jim, how was I going to get him out of that place? Hartshorn wouldn't even let me in the door. I had to take him."

"And wait a full year to let them know where Davy was."

"I don't have a lot of faith in people. Now tell me again what I'm supposed to do. I'll behave."

Jim smiled. "Believe in the system just a little and don't assume it's out to get you. For Davy's sake, Greg. It could make all the difference."

"And you don't think I need a sharp lawyer to go with me?"

"I truly believe that if you go into that courtroom and let the judge see that you're a good, decent man, you'll walk out with Davy. Anyway, I can't legally practice law in Pennsylvania, but I can advise you. You'll be

okay. I'll go over everything with you just before you leave, so you won't run into any surprises."

"I'd never forgive myself if I dropped the ball and ended up losing my boy."

"Any more cheery subjects on your mind? Say, how's the bed-and-breakfast business? I hear you had a good summer."

"Not bad. Ofelia made it happen by sheer Mexican willpower. Lord knows, I'm not the one with the personality."

"A bit rough at the edges, but likeable nonetheless. Got a full house today?"

"Slow week. There's one woman, that's all. How's your Anna—beautiful as ever?"

"Eight months pregnant and looks like an angel. What kind of woman did you lure to the old Seaview? A writer looking for atmosphere?"

"This one's doing public-opinion research."

"And . . . ?" Jim prodded.

"And nothing. She's nice."

"Young?"

"Not old."

"Good-looking?"

"Yes . . . very," he added after a pause.

"Uh-oh," Jim leaned back in his chair like an old family priest. "And here you are, ripe for picking."

"Dammit, Vargas!" Greg laughed and stood up. "I'm leaving before you make me mad."

"See you in a week or so. I'll get some things ready for you to look at. Stay loose, and I mean it."

Leslie gave an appreciative pat to the dark grandfather clock in the hall on her way out the front door. She steered her Mustang through the morning traffic, almost turning south on State Street toward the city college—toward Greg Austin—instead of north to the shopping mall.

She had a nine o'clock appointment with Ed and Dorothy Stone at the mall coffee shop to plan their strategy for the day. Ed and Dorothy were old hands at public relations, having had a small mail-order business for years. They'd recently sold out, and now in their late sixties, they were bored to death with retirement, itching to get out of the house and do something useful.

With their clipboards in hand, the three of them set forth into the busy mall to begin their survey work. People seemed interested in the questions, even eager to air their pet peeves, especially those concerning offensive ad layouts showing women in undignified situations. At this hour of the morning most of the shoppers were women with preschool-age children. Leslie wasn't allowed to show her personal feelings during a survey, but she did encourage people to elaborate on their complaints when she felt there was an important message to be sent back to the marketing strategists.

By noon the Stones had politely told her that they were doing just fine on their own and didn't need close supervision.

"I'm sure you could teach me a thing or two," Leslie agreed, and they smiled, knowing that they could.

"Why don't I check back at the end of the day and we can have a cup of something hot together?"

Leslie drove to the large supermarket where her team of housewives had set up a brightly decorated table in front of the entrance. No problems at all, they said, and showed her their thick pile of response forms and notes. Leslie stayed with them to observe their work for another hour, offering a few comments mostly to make herself feel she was useful. Justin had done such a good job of training his Santa Barbara team—and maybe she had done a good job of briefing them yesterday—that she was more of an observer than a close supervisor. She certainly didn't want to be looking over their shoulders every minute. It was important to allow them to take pride in doing well by themselves.

After grabbing a quick sandwich from the market's gourmet section, she drove to the city college to check on her student's team. They were working afternoons only, after their morning classes.

She found them in the area of the student center, swamped by friends who were noisily trying to register their opinions. The too-casual situation wasn't what Leslie wanted. Reluctantly she stepped in to restore some order. Because much of the paperwork was to be analyzed by computer it had to be done strictly by the book. Enthusiasm would have to be tempered by more attention to details.

This was going to take a little time to straighten out, and she wasn't unhappy at the prospect of staying on campus for the rest of the day. Leslie called on her knowledge of psychology to get her young team back on the track without losing their positive attitude toward the job.

But even as she was meticulously reviewing the procedures she was alert to the presence of Greg Austin. He was here somewhere; she could sense him nearby. When she caught herself thinking about him, she frowned. What was she doing, letting her contrary nature fire up like this just because an intriguingly natural man had come along?

A firm hand on her shoulder startled her. "Ofelia's back and you're invited to dinner," Greg said close to her ear.

When the fine hairs on the back of her neck had finally settled down, she managed to turn around. Her damned knees went weak at the sight of him. "I'd...I'd like that . . . very much," she said.

"Listen, if you still need victims for your survey, I'm available." His eyes held a twinkling playfulness. "I'll be good, I swear. I've had a pretty fair day, all things considered."

Leslie motioned to Jan, the auburn-haired coed who was trying very hard to develop a professional manner. "Jan, I have a subject for you—Dr. Austin. Just treat him the way you would any other person and try to get the most responses with the fewest questions."

Greg grinned. "Come on, Jan. Fire away with your toughest questions. We don't want to get on the wrong side of Miss O'Neill." He put his hands on his narrow hips and jutted out his beard-shadowed jaw with a wink in Leslie's direction. He had managed to put Jan at ease and steal Leslie's composure all at the same time. Maybe he wasn't the inexperienced country boy she had assumed he was. Or maybe it just came naturally to him—the body language, the intimate eye contact, the complicated timbre of his voice that carried so many possible meanings.

Leslie waited for her jumping nerves to settle down while she watched Jan earnestly recording Greg's every word and reaction to the advertising layouts. He was being a good sport, responding helpfully and completely, until he was shown a perfume ad with an elegantly dressed woman being kissed by one man as she flirted with another. "Trash," he said curtly.

"You don't think it's romantic?" Jan asked, taken aback by the sharpness of his response.

"Why should I? What man in his right mind would buy a perfume for a woman on the basis of that?" He stabbed a finger at the picture.

"It's more of a woman's fantasy," Leslie said, stepping in. "You weren't supposed to relate to it, just see the—"

"The possibilities? What's the name of that stuff?"

Jan looked pleadingly at Leslie. "How should I score his answer?"

Leslie shook her head. "That was a zero, Jan. Not only would the customer not buy it, he'd probably tell others not to, as well."

Greg smiled. "Nothing personal, ladies. You wanted honest opinions."

"Sure, Dr. Austin," Jan said. "Do you want to see any more?"

"Do I, Miss O'Neill?" Greg looked to Leslie for instructions. His eyes were playful again.

"Yes, you do. The rest of the questionnaire is harmless. I'll leave you two to finish. I've got to get back to the mall and meet with two of my team members. Remember, Jan, don't get rattled by belligerent subjects." She smiled straight at Greg.

"I'm a lamb," he said innocently and shrugged his broad shoulders so that his plaid flannel shirt strained for a moment against the hard muscles of his chest.

IT WAS SIX-THIRTY when Leslie finally dragged her feet up the white wooden steps of the Seaview Inn. She drew a deep breath of relief as she put her key into the front door lock. Ed and Dorothy Stone had talked her head off for the past two hours, proud of their first day and demanding that she hear every detail. She felt completely drained, and she blamed the pleasantly talkative old couple for the gnawing tightness in her stomach, instead of the fact that Greg Austin had managed to call up some frankly primitive responses in her by merely existing.

Ofelia met her in the hall, looking exactly as Leslie had imagined—short and stout, with large brown eyes and a genuinely welcoming smile. *"Señorita,"* she said as she put out a flour-flecked hand, *"Bienvenido a Santa Barbara!"* She wiped her hands quickly on her large yellow apron and apologized for them. "I make tortillas for dinner. Señor Austin is in his office—" she gestured behind her "—and Davy is outside. We will eat at seven o'clock, but you must sit on the porch before dinner and see our beautiful islands."

"Thanks, I will." Ofelia's personality was hard to resist.

"Señor Austin tells me you are a pretty woman be-cause I demand to know," she confided with a wink. "He's not so bad to look at, either, do you think?"

Leslie found herself nodding agreement. "Dinner smells wonderful," she said as she started up the stairs.

The upper landing of the house was quiet as usual—cool and peaceful. Leslie had the feeling of being in a time warp whenever she walked down from the sky-light of amber stained glass. It wouldn't be too surpris-ing to open her bedroom door one of these times and find herself in another century entirely.

She stepped inside her room, standing for a while on the friendly braided throw rug letting herself feel as if she belonged to the same era as the great oak armoire whose turned spindles nearly touched the ceiling. Just visible through the open bathroom door was the bulky claw-footed tub. And outside the windows she saw only a turquoise afternoon sky and the breeze-blown limbs of the sycamore tree—eternal things that belonged to any time in the past hundred years.

Her nostalgic mood ended abruptly when she checked her watch and lurched back to the present. Six-forty. There was still time before dinner to sit on the porch as Ofelia suggested to watch the Channel Is-lands and the setting sun.

The porch wrapped around the side of the house from the front to the parlor side, where an old-fashioned family swing hung invitingly. She sunk back into the generous cushions and wondered what it would be like to have this view every day of her busy life. Where she lived, there wasn't any porch, only a two-foot-wide balcony overlooking a noisy Hollywood street. And instead of a real house she had two rooms on the third floor of a sparkle-stucco apartment building.

Leslie caught a glimpse of Ofelia's cheery face as the woman passed by the parlor window. They both waved. The friendly creaking sounds of the swing as it moved on its orin frame acted as a natural tranquilizer. Far in the distance, sparkling in vivid clarity, lay the islands, not a wisp of fog or a cloud around them. They jutted from the cobalt sea like craggy dark green chunks of floating jade. Closer to shore, a dozen snow-white flecks moved slowly with the wind—sailboats returning to the harbor.

In the corner garden, where several rows of blooming roses glowed with the late sunlight, the little white gazebo cast complicated shadows from its white criss-crossed trellising. There was a delicious fragrance of eucalyptus drifting on the air, mixed with the heady smell of the sycamore.

Leslie tried to imprint this scene of beauty on her memory so she could draw it back at will. Ten days here and she might never want to return to L.A. She sighed and leaned far back into the deep, enveloping swing until her feet couldn't touch the ground and she was floating in its reassuring rhythm, her eyes closed.

The front door opened and shut. She heard footsteps coming along the porch in her direction, footsteps that could only be made by a man wearing boots.

"I come bearing guacamole and taco chips, compliments of Ofelia Reyes." Greg set two bowls down on the low table next to the swing. "I don't usually bother a guest who wants some privacy," he said with a smile that showed his even white teeth.

"It's no bother. I wasn't feeling exclusive."

"I have to be honest with you, Miss O'Neill. Ofelia sent me out here for purposes of her own."

Leslie looked at the rich green avocado dip and back at Greg. "She wants to make us both fat?" she teased.

"No. She thinks you're terrific and she almost pushed me out of the house to go and sit with you until dinner's ready." His smile showed that he wasn't an unwilling victim in the arrangement.

Leslie had to laugh. "I only just said hello to her a few minutes ago."

"I know, but she has a sixth sense about people. Anyway, here I am."

He stood there looking down at her, terribly appealing in his rumpled natural-toned cotton Western shirt and his tan twill pants. The turquoise inlay on his silver belt buckle was the same dappled sea green as his eyes. Leslie noticed that his face was clean shaven now. He looked a bit like a choir boy trying his best to be good.

"I think Ofelia has one eye out to see if I obeyed her," he continued.

"Well, I guess you should sit down, then," she said, making room for him on the swing. "Ofelia sent me out here, too," she admitted as she scooped up some of the spicy Mexican dip.

Greg stretched his arms over his head and crossed his long legs. "So how was your day?"

"Full," she replied, catching a sense-arousing hint of his special smell. It took an effort to be unaffected by his thighs brushing lightly against hers with the slow back and forth motion of the swing.

"Mine, too. My lawyer gave me a verbal thrashing at an early hour and I turned around and gave my students a hard time for the rest of the day. Pop quizzes for everyone," he admitted laughingly. "It takes the edge off the tension when you've got a lot on your mind."

"So you're one of those teachers who like to get their students rattled just for the fun of it?"

"Not at all." He grinned and reached around her to retrieve a handful of chips for himself. For a fleeting moment his face was very close to hers, and she became aware of the shape and texture of his lips.

"And what if I asked Ofelia about you?" she prodded, surprised at the teasing tone in her voice and wishing she had more control.

"Don't ask Ofelia unless you have an hour to kill hearing her say how bad it is that I'm not married, what an unnatural life I live . . . that sort of thing. I've got it all memorized."

Leslie smiled. "She sounds like my mother."

"Ofelia's one of those dear people who think we should all be marching two by two into the Ark. She gives every new female under fifty at the inn a good going-over." He shifted his body toward her so that one arm was draped casually over the back of the swing. In the motion his fingers accidentally grazed the back of her neck, and heat raced along her spine.

"And that's why I was invited to dinner tonight?" she asked.

"That's why. But don't let it worry you. Ofelia can't resist being hospitable. She also wants me to check you in before we eat, just to keep things straight with the government." He rose, brushing crumbs from his shirt.

Leslie tried to stand up, but fell back into the deep cushions.

Greg chuckled. "It's a trick swing. Here, take my hand."

She reached up to meet his firm, warm grip. Greg didn't release her as they walked back inside the house. "Just in case Ofelia's watching," he said with a wink and gave her hand a squeeze. Her knees went weak for the second time today. Was this low-key Robert Redford approach just a friendly California manner? Whatever it was, it felt too good to be good for her!

Just then, as the grandfather clock was striking seven and starting its Westminster chimes, Davy ran in from a side door with a slam and a breathless "Hi!"

"Clean hands, clean face, boy of mine," Greg ordered with a playful pat to Davy's rear end.

"Just fill this out and you're registered, Leslie," he said. "Or should I go back to Miss O'Neill?"

"Either one is fine," she answered, trying to pull back into a better state. She wasn't eager to play games, if this was a game.

"You can call *me* anything you want," he said, still sounding playful. He offered her his arm and they walked toward the source of the tantalizing cooking smells.

Ofelia burst through the kitchen door to the comfortable family dining room carrying a huge covered bean pot. "Sit down, Señor Austin—*señorita*... sit down," she urged. Davy came in smelling of soap and joined them at the round pine table.

Ofelia made several more trips until the table was arrayed with colorful serving dishes, and she finally sat down herself. "Chicken enchiladas, *frijoles refritos*, cilantro and *chile salsa*, my fresh corn tortillas, and *chiles rellenos*," she said, pointing to each steaming dish. "But first we take hands and say prayer for this food, *sí*?" She joined hands with Davy and Leslie. Greg took Leslie's other hand, finishing the little circle with Davy.

In the moment of silence around the table, Leslie couldn't think of a single prayer. Her left hand was being held by the hard-working hand of Ofelia—full of honest, loving warmth—and her other hand—firmly held by Greg—was tingling from the exchange of energy with him.

"Okay, let's eat," Greg said at last, removing his hand from hers.

Leslie knew that this was the best Mexican food she would ever eat, but she could barely taste the homemade tortillas or the biting hot tang of the salsa. Her nerves were on full alert to the man sitting beside her. He, however, seemed to be thoroughly enjoying his own meal.

Davy talked like a magpie through dinner, filling the air with a child's concerns such as problems with his friends on the schoolyard. Ofelia had to hush him to allow the adults some space, and then she directed the conversation to her own ends.

"*Señorita*, you are traveling alone. You are not married?" The probing black eyes had obviously noted that there was no wedding ring on her left hand.

"No, I'm not," Leslie replied, and a satisfied sound came from behind the napkin at Ofelia's lips.

"But the years go so fast, no? I married my first husband when I was sixteen. How old are you?"

"Old enough to know what she wants to do," Greg interrupted.

Serving Greg another large ladle of refried beans Ofelia retreated into silence, waiting for an apology.

"I'm sorry," Greg said, drawing a smile from her tightly compressed lips. "I'd guess that Miss O'Neill likes to choose her own time and place for things, and when she decides she's ready, that's it. No regrets. Am I right?" His eyes looked straight into Leslie's.

She nodded slowly, pleased by his perceptiveness. "I don't take risks without knowing there's a net below me. I've learned that much from experience."

He flashed a quick grin and tossed a warm tortilla onto her plate. "Every time I've jumped at something I've been sorry," he allowed, "but that doesn't mean I'm cured. I've been known to make a spectacular ass of myself from a hundred feet above the ground. No net in sight."

Leslie had to laugh. "I don't think you've done so badly."

"Just talk to my lawyer someday—he'll give you chapter and verse of my sins." With that he reached over to give Ofelia's hand a pat. "These enchiladas were the best I've had since you made them last week," he joked. Ofelia smiled broadly.

After dinner Greg helped Leslie from her chair and leaned close to her ear for a private word. "I apologize if I made you uncomfortable."

"Not at all," she protested. "I needed rescuing. Ofelia's very sweet, but . . ."

"You had my sympathy," he confided.

"Thanks." She turned around and almost met his lips, narrowly avoiding them with a quick awkward motion of her head that caused a rush of heat to her cheeks.

"It's nice to see women still blush," he said softly. "Good night, Leslie O'Neill."

AS SHE CLIMBED the stairs, Leslie's mind was racing with images that wouldn't go away. She couldn't recall ever having been so eager to do something as rash as exploring the intriguing character of Greg Austin.

She shed her clothes with a desperate urgency to bathe away the foolishness, the romantic fantasy. Good Lord, she caught herself, she wasn't in a time warp, she was in a brain warp!

The cool blue tiles of the bathroom floor felt good on her bare feet. She leaned far over the edge of the high tub to start the hot water and poured in a liberal dose of rosemary-scented bath oil.

It took a long time for the water level to come up. Leslie piled her hair into a knot at the top of her head and fetched her pink terry-cloth robe from the armoire. The bathroom was comfortably appointed, with thick towels of every size. The only thing it lacked was a stool for petite women guests to mount when entering the great lion-footed tub.

She sank slowly and blissfully into the water and let the scent of the rosemary oil carry away every tension in her body. Her breasts, partway out of the water, shimmered with little droplets of the aromatic oil and she was very much aware of herself as a woman. She watched an opaque swirl of oil slowly make a circle around her submerged abdomen, then scatter into little blobs.

The bathwater was cooling down and she shivered, reaching up with one glistening foot to turn the large white porcelain handle that had a big black *H* in the center. The water spat and groaned along the pipes, and Leslie smiled, thinking about the inn's antiquated plumbing system.

Suddenly she saw Greg standing in his soaked khaki work shirt yesterday morning. Another shiver moved through her. She was baffled to find herself so unreasonably drawn to a rough-hewn man; she had always thought she liked men who sent flowers and called a week in advance to make a date for the theater.

She smiled at herself and reached for a large, fluffy white bath towel. What would Justin advise? "Take two Bach quintets with a good cognac and call me in the morning. If you're still crazy, you'll get my favorite lecture on confusing excitement with real life."

She felt almost euphoric, her body just a little tingly moving beneath the soft abrasion of the towel as she returned to her bedroom. While she had bathed, someone had turned down her bed covers and left a foil-wrapped mint on her lacy pillow. She claimed her nighttime treat and mentally thanked Ofelia; it was good to be coddled and cared for, with nothing expected in return.

While the delicious chocolate mint melted slowly in her mouth, she opened the oak-paneled armoire doors and stood staring at her modest assortment of clothes, planning for tomorrow.

A knock at the door was followed by Greg's booming voice. "I'm on my way down the hall to play host to a gentleman who just checked in. Is it too late for your glass of sherry?"

Leslie put her hand up to check the security of her towel sarong and opened the door a crack. "It's not too late," she said, feeling unabashed pleasure at the sight of him. He was balancing a small round tray with two liqueur glasses.

"I'll be back in a minute...unless you want me to just leave it," he offered.

"No," she said quickly. "I'll wait for you."

"I'd hoped you'd say that. Back in a bit." He grinned at her and closed the door behind him.

Leslie whipped off the towel and thought of dressing again, but that was silly at this hour. Her mulberry silk nightgown was as modest as most dresses she owned, anyway, except for the candlelight lace over the bodice. The terry-cloth robe would cover any lack of discretion in the nightgown. With an unsteady hand she pulled a comb through her heavy damp hair.

Tying the sash of the robe loosely around her waist, she reached for her work notes and sat down in the low Victorian rocking chair, forcing her eyes from the door and onto her opinion surveys. The tingling sensation on the surface of her well-scrubbed skin had all moved to a very definite spot in the pit of her stomach. All at once she felt very foolish. This fascination with Greg had to be a silly rebellion against Derek's managing of her life. It certainly didn't make sense otherwise, and she wasn't very pleased with herself.

Greg knocked again and waited for her to let him in. There were still two full glasses on the silver tray. "My new guest down the hall is a teetotaler. I would have been back sooner, but I had to listen politely to a lecture about the evils of alcohol. Anyway, he loved the mint."

"I won't lecture you," Leslie said.

"That's a relief. It's been a day full of nice people telling me I'm doing things wrong." His broad smile brought deep crevices to the corners of his eyes and around his mouth.

"But you did give poor Jan a hard time with her survey," she reminded him gently. "That's all I'll say."

"You changed out of your towel," he observed as he handed her one of the sherry glasses.

"I feel more comfortable this way," she said, meeting his heady masculine presence with a smile.

His green eyes flickered slightly in response as he touched his glass to hers with a clink. "I'm all for comfort. Cheers." He downed the contents of his glass while he watched her.

"Cheers," she answered, fascinated by his penetrating gaze that managed to see around and through her and still appear as innocent as a baby's. She sat down again in the rocking chair, making a reasonably graceful descent. "And thanks for the rosemary oil. I had a glorious bath just now."

"I can tell. I have a weakness for the fresh plant smell. It reminds me of the Santa Ynez Mountains in the heat of summer. Did you know that the Chumash Indians used rosemary to chase away evil spirits?"

Leslie shook her head cautiously. "Who were the Chumash Indians?" She didn't want to be the butt of some joke he was making.

"This was once their land—the coastline and the hills. Now all that's left are broken pots and grinding stones and some incredible painted caves in the hills behind us. I've discovered a few myself that the archaeologists don't know about yet, in the rough country back toward Ventura. Untouched and pristine, with colors as clear as the day they were painted, maybe a thousand years ago. I'm happy when I'm up there with my caves." His voice was warm with feeling, and Leslie was caught up in the spell he had woven.

"I envy you," she said, meaning it.

Greg looked down at her for a long silent moment, then leaned close to smooth back a fallen lock of her damp hair with one of his large hands. "I'll take you up there someday, if you'd like." He seemed about to say something more, but stopped himself. "Now I'd better go tuck Davy in for the night." He quickly picked up his tray and glass and almost bolted to the door without another word, leaving Leslie to sort out what had just happened between them.

"Good night to you, too," she said under her breath. In a way she was glad he was gone. She heard his heavy footsteps on the stairs, but the essence of his energy was still with her in the room, potent and compelling, like a force of nature.

Greg Austin was unique, she had to admit. It would take some effort to ignore him, with his gingerbread house and mysterious Indian caves and hypnotic green eyes.

As she lifted the sherry glass to her lips, she heard a peculiar groaning sound coming from behind the wall near the door, followed by a thud and a shudder that vibrated through the floor. Were the old pipes about to burst? Curious, she went to the door and looked out into the hallway. It was empty and silent. A loud thud sounded again, very close this time, and she whirled about, but all she saw was the blank wall next to her.

Then a small hand slid out from between two sections of wall paneling and a voice whispered, "It's me . . . Davy. Don't tell my dad where I am." His face could be seen in the partly opened panel door.

Leslie crouched to open the small door all the way. "What are you doing in there?" she asked. "And what on earth is this thing?"

"The dumbwaiter," Davy whispered. He was sitting with his knees up under his chin looking like a naughty elf. The dumbwaiter was a large wooden cabinet that functioned like a miniature elevator. Leslie had never seen one, but she knew that many older houses had had them to carry food trays to their upper floors.

She laughed. "Don't you think you're being silly? Your father's looking for you right now. I'll bet you're not supposed to be joyriding in his dumbwaiter."

"I do it all the time," he said, and suddenly dropped from sight with a whoosh and a screeching of ropes and pulleys. His flushed face looked startled.

"Davy, are you all right?" she called down into the dark, musty silence of the shaft. "Answer me."

A moment later the dumbwaiter rattled back up, but Davy wasn't inside. Leslie leaned as far as she dared into the empty compartment. "Davy?"

"Come on down," his high voice echoed from far away, "it's fun."

"Grown-ups don't do things like that," she said in her firmest voice. "I think you'd better come right back up here." She heard muffled giggling and the machinery started once more. Down plunged the dumbwaiter to the bottom and after a pause, up again, groaning on its thick ropes. Leslie reached to open the door, but her hand was seized and held by a very large hand—not a child's. She let out an involuntary cry and jumped away while Greg unfolded his tall body from the cramped compartment.

"I couldn't help it," he said, laughing at her surprise. "I went down to the basement to look for the little scamp and found out what he was up to. So I brought him back down, ready to give his bottom a good swat. Then I heard you saying what grown-ups do and don't do, and I had this crazy urge to climb in myself. I swear, I don't know what got into me. Are you okay?"

Leslie let out an exasperated breath and had to laugh. "You're as bad as your little boy, Mr. Austin. Have compassion for a stranger and tell me what other secrets this old house has. I don't want to be falling through trapdoors or disappearing behind hidden bookcases."

"That's all we have. A barn owl or two under the eaves, and some critters in the attic, but nothing to worry about." His eyes were playful, with green turbulence just underneath. "I hope this whole thing didn't upset you. Davy and I were just in a wild mood."

"You aren't going to spank him, are you?"

"Not now. I never was good at it, not while I still have so much orneriness in myself. He's just an Austin, and there's no cure for that." He grinned. "Anyway, I used to do things as a boy that would curl your hair."

"Like what?" she found herself asking. She leaned against the wall next to the dumbwaiter and folded her arms across her chest.

"Oh, Lordy!" he chuckled. "One time my mother was in the kitchen canning a whole summer's worth of peaches and I thought it would be the funniest thing in the world to let loose a skunk and see what happened. Well, the skunk was scared and so was my mother, and you can guess what went on in the next ten seconds. Hot peach syrup everywhere, skunk spray and yelling . . . It was awful."

"No!" Leslie laughed. "What happened to you then?"

He made a pained face. "My parents took turns with the belt and the hairbrush. I had to clean up the mess, too. I probably deserved worse. Dad was a country doctor for a lot of the ranch families in Ventura County. He was the kind who didn't mind driving in the middle of the night to tend a sick child. Everything I know about fathering came from him—the good part, anyway."

"Davy's a lucky boy," Leslie said softly.

"Thanks, I needed to hear that."

There was an awkward silence. "Well, good night again." Leslie extended her hand to him. "I'm really glad I discovered the Seaview Inn. Any other place wouldn't be half as much fun."

He took her hand and regarded her for a moment, as if deciding whether to say his next words. "I'm glad you found the Seaview, too, and I have a confession to make. Before I came to your room this evening I almost dropped the sherry glass in that old man's lap, I was in such a blazing rush to see you again. And when I did, all I could talk about was my Indian caves. Then the next time you see me I'm sitting in my dumbwaiter. You must have a hell of a sense of humor. Not many women—" He stopped, realizing he was squeezing her hand too tightly. "Anyway, thanks for putting up with all of us." He brought her hand up to his lips and kissed it before letting it go. "I'm not always so clumsy," he added with an odd smile that for a moment revealed an intensity that Leslie wasn't comfortable to perceive.

5

A SHAFT OF DAWN LIGHT angled through the side window and moved across the foot of Leslie's bed like a warm silent finger. She hadn't slept well. Greg's energy had swirled around her like a current, upsetting her inner balance.

Breakfast was a long time off yet, and further sleep was impossible. She slipped from bed, reaching for a blank notebook and soft pencil. Ever since she'd first set eyes on this house she had wanted to make sketches of the Victorian scrollwork around the old window-frames and doors. She had noticed one window in particular, at the end of the upstairs hall.

With her robe tied snugly around her, she left her room. The hallway was dimly lit by two antique brass wall sconces. She walked the length of the hallway. The beveled and leaded glass window was graceful in a way that few modern designs were; it framed a good view of the side garden of the inn.

She was doing a quick sketch when something outside caught her attention. There, in the misty morning light she saw the figure of a tall man—Greg. He was splitting logs with an obvious fury that took her breath away. The log seemed more like an enemy than a harmless piece of eucalyptus. Again and again he brought the ax down.

Leslie hurried away from the scene, feeling like an intruder. A few minutes later, from the sanctuary of her room, she heard the Jeep make a crunching turn-around in the driveway and, with grinding gears, accelerate fast onto Anacapa. She watched the empty street, wishing she could stop reacting to absolutely everything this man did.

She took the time before breakfast to transcribe notes from her tape recorder, using the small electronic type-writer that fitted into her briefcase. Derek had laughed at her executive look. "What next?" he had asked, "a telephone for your car? Is your beeper going to go off during our intimate moments?"

"Our intimate moments," she mused and set the typing aside. How strangely joyless their lovemaking had been, how empty of real loving. She couldn't forgive herself for such poor judgment, or for letting him think that marriage had ever been a possibility.

She dressed for her third day of work, choosing a rose-toned cotton shirtwaist dress, yet another garment district discovery. Justin was the only man she should be thinking about today. She wanted more than anything else to do a good job for him. Suddenly understanding his amusement about "all the fuss and thunder" of romance, she managed a smile.

At seven-thirty she went downstairs. Ofelia was in the kitchen with Davy and a tall, cadaverously thin older man who was blooming under Ofelia's generous attentions.

"My dad's gone out," Davy said through a mouthful of cereal. "He's up at the cabin."

"He doesn't have classes today?" Leslie asked, curious in spite of herself.

Ofelia greeted her with a friendly pat on the shoulder and served her a steaming portion of eggs scrambled with onions and bits of green cactus. "Señor Austin does not work on Friday. He has many things on his mind now. The cabin is where he thinks." She gave Leslie an intent look with her eloquent brown eyes. "Maybe you understand, *sí*?"

The new guest leaned over the breakfast table to extend a formal hand. "Arthur Blaine," he said. "Happy to meet a fellow traveler." His pale grin and ever paler blue eyes gave him the look of a man who rarely ventured beyond his account books or the inner stacks of a library. "This kind lady tells me you have important business here in Santa Barbara." He inclined his head toward Ofelia. "I'm a history buff myself—the Spanish missions. You know, of course, that Santa Barbara was the first mission to be founded after the death of Father Serra. Such history, such passion in these old places," he said with a little wheeze of emotion.

"I'm Leslie O'Neill," she offered with a smile, "and my work doesn't sound half as interesting as yours. I do opinion research." She went back to enjoying her eggs and fresh warm tortillas and sour cream. "Davy," she said between bites, "what do you like to do best when you don't have school?"

His freckled face lit up as he swallowed a huge gulp of milk. "I like to see the animals at the zoo and I like to go with my dad up to the caves."

"The Indian caves? Are they nice?"

"Yeah," he said appreciatively. "Dad and me just sit there and look at those funny pictures on the walls—bugs and snakes and stuff." He looked serious and Leslie stifled a smile.

Ofelia crossed herself quickly. "They were not Christians, those old ones who make magic in the caves."

"In my studies I *have* found some irregular practices—distressing." The gentleman shook his head regretfully.

"The Indians aren't so bad as all that," Davy insisted.

Mr. Blaine smiled tolerantly. "The missions did fine work bringing the heathens out of their darkness."

Davy's face clouded. He might not have understood the words, but apparently he knew the Indians were being maligned. "My dad knows all about the Chumash and he says—"

"What if I can get some time Saturday to take you to the zoo?" Leslie interrupted hastily. "Do you think that would be all right with your father?"

The boy's belligerence evaporated and he smiled. "Sure! Then I can show you the lion and the monkeys and all the birds. I'll show you everything!"

Mr. Blaine dabbed his lips with his napkin and stood up. "I'll be spending the day with the good fathers at the mission and in their library. It has been a pleasure, ladies."

"How are you going to get to school?" Leslie asked Davy.

"The bus. I have to get there real early and stand around with the other kids. I like it better when my dad drives me, 'cause we talk about things." With that he left the table, snatched his lunch bag and gave Ofelia a kiss on the cheek in passing. "See ya later." He started for the swinging door to the main hall and up the stairs to the tower.

"Let me pour another cup of coffee," Ofelia said. "If you have few minutes to talk, okay?"

"Thanks."

She set the steaming pot down again and sat in the chair opposite Leslie. "Davy is a sweet boy, don't you think?"

"He's great. I can see his father in him already."

Ofelia was silent for a while, sipping her coffee. "Do you know about the big trouble, *señorita*?"

Leslie looked up cautiously. "What trouble?"

She leaned closer and confided, "I tell you a story." Leslie wasn't sure she wanted to hear this, but Ofelia continued.

"Many years ago Señor Austin fall in love with a beautiful girl and he marry her, very fast. He was working hard to finish his doctor's study and he did not know what he was doing to have a fast romance like that." She cocked an eye to see if Leslie was following.

"This girl . . . Celeste . . . come from a rich family in Philadelphia. Her father is in the business of big ships that carry oil . . ."

"Tankers?" Leslie supplied.

"*Sí*. And this Señor Hartshorn, he put Señor Austin behind a desk in a tall building to work for him. And for a long time he is unhappy."

"I'm sorry." This was getting uncomfortable, Leslie thought.

"And then Celeste is pregnant and Davy come."

Leslie nodded and checked her watch, hoping for an excuse to leave.

"But Celeste is selfish and give Davy to the nursemaid so she can travel and have parties. A very bad woman." Ofelia grimaced. "Señor Austin work hard in his tall building, and one day he come home and Celeste is with another man. In bed, *señorita!* What do you think Señor Austin feel now? It is very bad. Not one man, one time, but many men, many times—and she laugh at Señor Austin."

"I'm really sorry, but—" Leslie started to leave.

Ofelia put out a hand to stop her. "And then, you know what happen? Señor Austin make papers for separation and he go away for a little time. His heart is breaking. How can a man live with such a thing?" She crossed herself. "Then one night, when she is out having parties with her friends, there is a car crash and Celeste is dead. Just like that." She snapped her fingers. "And now you know what?" She gripped Leslie's wrist. "Now the mother and father of Celeste try to take Davy."

ven the most difficult people into willing subjects by
heer force of kindness, and her two housewives had
lready run out of questionnaires. "Fantastic!" she
yped into her little machine, then pressed the erase tab
nd watched the word disappear.

She spent much of the afternoon with Jan and Allen,
udging them into adopting a semiprofessional style.
At the end of the day, she gave Jan a ride back to her
amily's house, then on a whim invited her to have
dinner in town.

"I'd love to, Miss O'Neill, but my boyfriend's wait-
ng to take me out." She was apologetic, and Leslie
uddenly felt old compared to this perky girl who was
only five or six years younger than she was.

"Maybe another time, okay?" Jan offered.

Leslie smiled. "I forgot it was Friday night. We'll do
t next week, then." She let Jan off and drove slowly
down the narrow winding road above the mission. She
vanted to do something tonight, but what? Six months
vith Derek had made her used to companionship,
vrong as it was. That dependency was something she
ad to work on.

The meandering drive took her past the Natural
History Museum. She stopped near the entrance sign,
ut it was already past closing time. In her glove com-
artment she found her tourist guide to Santa Barbara.
With all its vaunted history and delights, there had to
e something for her to see or do in this town.

Running her eyes down the list of historical places,
he ruled out the mission—too serious. The Botanic
Gardens would be closed now, and she wouldn't visit

Leslie snapped to attention. "That's terrible!"

"In three weeks—not even three—Señor Austin and
Davy must go to Philadelphia and the judge will say if
Davy come back to us again." Tears welled in her eyes
and spilled over. "Maybe we lose Davy."

"But there are laws. They can't just take a child."

"Señor Hartshorn is very rich and Señor Austin is
not. Rich people can get whatever they want."

"No," Leslie contradicted. "That's not how it is in this
country. Rich people have to obey laws, too."

"They promise to send Davy to private school and
give him things. Señor Austin cannot do this." She
shrugged.

"It will work out, I'm sure." It was Leslie's turn to take
Ofelia's hand.

"Pray to God, I hope so. But a little boy need more
than just a father. He need a mother, too. Maybe the
judge say that. I don't know."

"Anyone can see that Mr. Austin is a good father.
He'll win."

Ofelia looked intently at Leslie after a pause. "A lot
of women, they like Señor Austin, you know? But I
think he's going to wait too long...and everybody will
be gone. Fast romance is bad, but slow romance is not
so good, either, you know what I mean?"

Leslie put down her cup and stood to leave. "I don't
know very much about that sort of thing." She smiled
back at Ofelia's probing eyes. "But I do know I'm a
working lady who shouldn't spend any more time over
coffee. Thanks for breakfast. It was great."

Ofelia watched her go. "Have a nice day," she called.

Davy ran past Leslie in the front hall on his way out the door. "See ya," he said.

She smiled and responded "See ya" to the departing back already halfway down the front steps. How in the world had she landed in this wonderful madhouse? Tears tipped over onto her cheeks, and she didn't try to stop them.

GREG SHIFTED the Jeep into four-wheel drive and felt the surge of power as it started up the rough fire road toward the cabin. He checked the back to see if his load of wood was secure; he might need this supply to see him through the winter. He might just be spending a lot of weekends up here—if he didn't have Davy anymore.

And why had fate dropped Leslie O'Neill into his lap just now, of all times, he wondered, with that soft voice that went straight to his gut, those brown eyes and that little smile. He didn't even remember how to act with a woman like that; it had been so long since he'd let himself care.

There was so much churning momentum inside him already from the few times he'd been alone with her. What was that supposed to mean? He cringed thinking of the women he'd known since Celeste. He hated that kind of life, hated what it had done to him while he'd played the eligible bachelor all over Santa Barbara. But that was behind him. All he wanted now was to be left alone with Davy and what little peace of mind he could muster.

So what about this new woman? His loud, laugh filled the air. He had a feeling that fate going to let him get away with anything anymo a thing.

LESLIE CAUGHT a draft of fresh sweet air as slammed the door behind him. He was a charm tle heathen—even Mr. Blaine would have to agr could picture Greg and Davy sitting in their Indi far from civilization and dreaming about the day the earth talked to humans, and the bugs and sn the painted walls had some deep meaning.

The grandfather clock solemnly chimed t hour. She would miss this place after next wee she would always wonder what was happenin man with the autumn green eyes.

She deliberately turned her attention to ahead. Friday would be a busy time at the sl malls and the supermarkets, but in the afterno college campus around would be deserted. Sl her two students, Jan and Allen, relieved to ca before they left for class, diverting them for t noon to a small shopping center east of town.

The day turned out to be hectic. Leslie div time between the large mall, two widely sepa permarkets and Jan and Allen's station to the lunch hour was spent in a mall parking lot v grabbed a takeout bean sprout sandwich. He serving as a temporary office. Typewriter or she put her own notes into proper form, v pleased with her team. The retired couple wa

the zoo, which was reserved for tomorrow with Davy. The beach was famous for its wide expanse of sand and its gentle surf, but she wasn't dressed for a seaside stroll. She read on: "The luxurious Biltmore Hotel has lured the discerning traveler to Santa Barbara since the twenties, contributing to the city's reputation for romance and glamour."

A simple movie and dinner at a decent restaurant in town would do fine. She closed the guidebook and returned it to the glove compartment. Derek's folded message fell out, along with the little cocktail coaster. She let them lie where they'd landed. She didn't want to see the bold handwriting again with its command that she remember their night at the Coronado. Of course she remembered, but that was all; it was a memory, fading fast along with all those other nights they'd shared.

The movie she chose was a dark French drama about suspicious, vengeful lovers hopelessly racked by their own wild passions, and most happy when they were punishing each other. Not what she needed tonight, she concluded. With an impatient grunt, she left her seat and stumbled through the dim, flickering light past several people and out into the lobby, where she bought a large box of buttered popcorn and left the theater.

Her dinner, which she'd eaten in haste at an Italian restaurant, was already sitting uneasily in her stomach, and the popcorn was the last straw. By the time she reached the Seaview, she had a full-blown headache and worse.

Waiting for her on her bedside table was a special courier packet from Olson and Loeb, from the desk of Justin Reiner.

"Forgive me, Justin," she groaned, "but I just have to lie down first." Her mind was swimming. Even the muted lamplight was too much right now. Lying in the soothing darkness she drifted to sleep.

Later she woke up, not sure which end of the day it was, evening or predawn. The house was quiet. She squinted, switching on the light, then saw that it was only ten-thirty. Mercifully, the headache was gone, her mind was clearer and she was ready to see what Justin had sent her in the important-looking manila envelope.

She sighed as she read the closely typed pages; they listed changes in the questionnaire . . . lots of them. Apparently, they'd taken on a big new account—men's cosmetics.

A large folder contained photo layouts of the Bon Homme advertising campaign in several versions. Leslie studied the pictures of the male models. The idea intruded that Greg Austin was as ruggedly handsome as any of them, and probably more of a real man.

Leslie's wayward thoughts ceased when she read Justin's postscript: "I'm forwarding a letter from your young man. Your love life puts me in an awkward position, Leslie. I do hope you straighten it out soon."

What had Derek done now? Leslie fished around at the bottom of the large mailer and found the elegant envelope that she knew so well. She had been with Derek at Bullock's Wilshire when he ordered his stationery. Resigned she took a deep breath and ran her finger under the flap to remove the letter.

Darling,
I hope this finds you well and happy. I'm honoring your desire for isolation, even though one of the investigators here at the office found you in a matter of hours. Give me credit for that, love.

These past few days haven't been pleasant for me, to say the least, wondering how much time is enough time for a woman to come to her senses.

Next Tuesday evening I will have reserved one of the garden cottages at the Biltmore Hotel, not far from where you are hiding. I have also bought two tickets on the Concorde to Europe and booked a two-week stay at an eighteenth-century villa high on a cliff overlooking the sea in Sorrento. You'll love the Amalfi coast.

I decided that we need to get away together and plan our future in the best atmosphere. We'll leave the day you get back to L.A. I've already cleared our plans with Justin Reiner, who seems to understand these things. Tuesday, then. I'll be in the Biltmore bar at 7:30. I love you.

Derek

Leslie didn't know whether to laugh or cry. Who wouldn't love to fly to Europe and stay in one of the most romantic spots in Italy? But what presumption, to talk to Justin first, and then buy tickets!

She crumpled the letter and hurled it across the room.

She stormed to the armoire, pulled out her old jeans and gym socks and her bulky Berber wool pullover sweater. She needed a good run somewhere... anywhere. She jammed her feet into a pair of blue sneakers and tied a scarf over her hair.

"Damn!" she breathed as she left the room. She almost stumbled over the little tray with the mint and liqueur glass that had been left beside her door. A neatly printed card was propped against the glass: "*Buenas noches.* We didn't wish to disturb you." Ofelia's name was written underneath.

In one quick motion she bent to take the glass and mint, swallowing the sherry and putting the mint into her pants pocket before hurrying down the steps and out the front door. Behind her the hall clock was marking the quarter hour; ahead of her the crisp blue-black night beckoned.

6

SHE STRODE FAST along the crunching gravel of the driveway and out onto the sidewalk. The one-two, one-two rhythm of her legs quickly reached a jog, and by the end of two blocks she began to feel that special sensation of muscles stretching to their capacity. She hadn't been jogging for weeks. Her breath came evenly, but the cool night air bit into the back of her throat; the pain felt good.

She was running uphill on Anacapa, forcing her full attention to the effort when headlights slowly approached her on the deserted street. Greg's Jeep eased to a stop at the curb next to her, and she too, stopped.

"I didn't recognize you at first," he said. "Need a lift?"

"No, thanks. I'm just out for some air," she panted.

"Looks more like an endurance run."

"I need it." She started moving again, and Greg backed the Jeep alongside her, keeping pace.

"This is a nice neighborhood, but I don't recommend it for a lone woman at this hour of the night. Hop in. I'll find you a better place."

She stopped again, trying to catch her breath while he waited, grinning at her. In the semidarkness his face glinted with a day's growth of blond beard. His moonlit, perceptive eyes melted her truculence and she gave in. "All right. But I warn you, I'm not great company."

Greg smiled against her resistance. "We'll see about that. Get in." She climbed into the car and arranged her legs around the toolbox, not caring this time if there were unspeakable things on the seat to soil her clothes.

Greg jammed the Jeep into low gear. "You would have run into a pack of rowdy teenagers two blocks up."

"I can handle myself."

"Right. I forgot, you're tough." His friendliness was disarming. She didn't want to be cheered up.

"Now, where shall I take you?" he continued. "How about a run on the beach? I haven't done that for a while."

She was beginning to tingle from his nearness, and before she knew it she had said yes. "I'm not much of a runner, though. I'm really out of shape."

He turned and smiled at her, the creases at the corners of his eyes and lips adding to his charm. "I won't comment on what shape you're in."

The Jeep hurtled down Anacapa and turned ontc Shoreline Drive where they parked. A few flickering campfires dotted the broad beach close to the sidewalk. "How about two miles at an easy lope and two miles back at a walk?"

"If you hear me saying uncle, have mercy on me," she replied.

They walked past the scattering groups near the barbecues and started running just above the waterline where the sand was moist and hard. The huge full moon overhead gave everything a silver tint.

"It's good for you, Miss O'Neill. Gets the brain cells working." He took her hand and set a slow pace, reining in his long stride to match her shorter one. The feel of his hand brought back the disconcerting sense of belonging that she was hoping had been just a figment of her imagination.

The tang of the sea air was stimulating, but soon she was panting. "How much farther?" She was starting to feel just how out of shape her legs were.

"Not far. East Beach ends just before we get to the Biltmore. Maybe a half mile more. Saying uncle?"

"No. I can make it."

The tide was high, forcing them to scramble over a long outcropping of rocks. Leslie suddenly sat down hard on one of them. "That's it. Not another step. I need a minute to catch my breath."

"Take off your shoes and let your feet dangle in the tide pools. After they get numb, they'll start to feel warm again," he said sympathetically.

She dangled her feet in the still pools between the rocks. "I'm glad you picked me up tonight," she admitted. "I was in a rotten mood."

"Problems with your work?"

"Work is fine; in fact, it's the only thing that is." She didn't look at him but into the little pool, probing with her big toe in the wet sand.

"I won't get personal. My life's nothing to brag about right now, either."

Leslie smiled. "Ofelia told me about Señor Austin's big problem this morning. I'm really sorry."

"I imagine she told you everything—all the gruesome details."

"Pretty much, I'm afraid. I didn't want her to tell me, really. She just did."

"Ofelia talks too much, but her heart's as big as the sky."

"She obviously loves you and Davy."

"It's the best kind of love, with no twists or turns," he confirmed.

"I like Davy a lot. He's opinionated for a child. He gave old Mr. Blaine a hard time at breakfast."

Greg threw back his head and laughed when Leslie related the conversation. The breeze tousled his blond hair until he looked as young as his son. "As long as Davy's with me he won't grow up shy."

"Ofelia said something about you being at a cabin," Leslie ventured.

He nodded slowly. "My place of sanity. Nine years ago when I was doing field work for my doctorate I built a cabin in the middle of the area I was mapping, way back up in the Santa Ynez Mountains. You'd probably call it a shack, but I've done a lot of good thinking there. I lived there for six months while I did the mapping. Probably the happiest time of my life. Right after that everything changed and I got married. I guess you know the rest."

Leslie shrugged in sympathy. "We all get tangled up at one time or another," she said, thinking about her own shaky state.

"Now, since you already know so much about me, it's only right that I know more about you. Or you could just tell me to go jump."

Leslie could feel his playful eyes on her, daring her to refuse his honest offer. "There's not much to tell, except that I've learned more than I wanted to know about being bullied."

"And?" he prodded with his rich, low voice, and took hold of her hand.

"There's a man I was close to in Los Angeles, who expected to marry me. I was feeling guilty for breaking off with him until . . ." She looked down at their hands and saw him smiling at her. "Until I opened an irritating letter he wrote me. As soon as I threw it against the wall I felt free, completely free for the first time."

"Do I deserve to hear more?"

"Probably not," she said. "I wish him well, but not with me. If he keeps on refusing to believe it, that's his problem, not mine." She let out a long, exasperated sigh, then looked up and found Greg's eyes intently scanning her face.

"There's something I've been wanting to do, Miss O'Neill," he whispered so softly that she almost didn't hear his words. Then he leaned closer and their lips touched—gently, tentatively, warmly. "I'm glad you're free."

In the long, wonderful moment Leslie kissed him back, loving the sensation of his welcoming lips, the heat of his body close to hers, the masculine scent of him mixed with the whipping sea winds that caught both of them up in a cloak of excitement.

Greg's hand drew a slow line of fire across her cheek and lips, stopping at her chin to tilt her face upward for his scrutiny. "Why do I have such a hell of a time around you? I fell like I'm twelve years old and that was my first awkward kiss. Would you like to do it again?" His grin was irresistible.

This time she came to him, watching as he tantalizingly brushed his lips against hers, refusing her more than those brief, promising touches until at last he parted his lips and sent his eager tongue toward hers in the first stunning contact. The charged silence was punctuated only by the natural sounds of wind and waves. They plunged into their new world of delights, exploring the smooth inner landscapes of the kiss, advancing and then retreating until there was nowhere to go but further into new and dangerous territory. The moon hung high in the sky, washing them with its intoxicating glow, suspending them for a time in a separate reality.

Suddenly Greg pulled away. "I think that's enough nourishment for the walk back," he whispered roughly and stood up, drawing her with him. Leslie couldn't speak. She was grateful that his words had ended their startlingly passionate embrace, but she was dizzy from the power of it. Her hand went out toward him and his fingers laced through hers. Walking ankle-deep in the lapping tide with their shoes slung over their shoulders, they didn't speak for a long time.

"Her name was Celeste," Greg said at last.

"I know."

He thought a while, then grunted a little laugh. "I'm glad my folks didn't live long enough to see how our marriage turned out. You were smart to get out of your situation before it was too late."

"I shouldn't be angry with Derek. He never did anything terrible to me, except be himself. That was my fault, for not wanting to see."

"I suppose Derek's a go-getter, with big plans for success."

She smiled at the understatement. "Big plans. And I was supposed to smile sweetly and go along with them."

"Any man can see you're not the type to be put into a mold," he commented.

"I'm certainly not going to get married just because it's the reasonable thing to do. But your own marriage wasn't all bad, was it? Weren't there times . . . ?"

"If I hadn't married Celeste I wouldn't have had Davy. Maybe that's what it was all for. I don't know. And if I hadn't been an ass about a lot of things, I wouldn't be fighting to keep him." He dredged up a half smile with his sensitive, mobile lips. "I shouldn't be dumping my problems on you. But Davy doesn't *belong* in a Philadelphia mansion where they don't let you track a little mud on the floor. I want him to be a real person." They reached the car and Greg opened the door for her. "That's my last growl for the night, I promise."

"You're a nice man, Greg," she said softly. Her voice caught in her throat. "If . . . if there's anything I can do to help . . . you and Davy . . ."

He leaned down and cradled her face in his large warm hands, kissing her very tenderly. "Thanks." He walked around to the driver's side and started the car. While the engine was noisily idling, he handed her a towel for her sandy feet and said, "You're not so bad yourself. Don't let me complain like that again. I swore I was going to do this thing right with the custody case. I'm doing my damnedest to curb my temper. Lawyer's orders." He gunned the Jeep backward onto the nearly empty coast road.

"Where are we going?" Leslie checked her watch; it was after one o'clock.

"I don't want to take you home just yet. Is that all right?" His tone was hopeful.

"It depends. In five hours I have to start overhauling my entire survey, retrain my team and try out the new format all over town. And then I'm taking Davy to the zoo. By that time I'll belong in a zoo!" She laughed.

"What I have in mind will make up for any lost sleep."

"You sound sure of that," she said cautiously, not wanting to go home right now, either.

"You're about to have a guided tour of the Botanic Gardens by moonlight." He turned the car northward and drove through the sleeping city.

"Isn't it closed at this hour? That's what my little book says."

He laughed. "It is closed to the public, but I give field trips there, and the board of trustees is used to my eccentric habits." They passed the old mission, with its bright pink columns lit by both moonlight and man-made light, then curved up the road, going deeper into the pungent-smelling wild hills.

"That's mountain sage," Greg told her; he sounded contented. "The smell makes me feel alive." Shadowy gnarled sycamores loomed and receded. Remnants of old olive groves dotted the roadside fields.

Greg turned off the road and parked near the entrance to the gardens. A night bird shrilled a high call from a nearby tree and was answered by another. "The sounds of the night," Greg whispered. "Do you know what bird that was?"

Leslie shook her head. "I know it's not an owl. What is it?"

"I'll let you read a paper I wrote on the night-bird calls of California. It'll be good for you, city girl."

"Don't be condescending," she retorted. "In my own territory, I'm tops."

"Come on, I want to show you a very special place." He opened the car door and stepped out.

Leslie slid out on Greg's side. Her knees were feeling the effects of the long jog on the beach, and her upper leg muscles were weak.

He took her hand and started to walk. "How about a stroll in the most beautiful canyon in the world?"

Leslie could feel the change of atmosphere as soon as they entered the gardens. In the soft balmy air the startlingly bright moon cast a shimmer over the earthen trail. Acorns crunched underfoot. Little scuttling sounds and sudden rustles of birds taking flight from trees told her that she was intruding.

"It seems like a thousand eyes are watching us," she whispered as they picked their way along a gently sloping area sprinkled with desert plants and scrub growth. Trees towered above them and the air felt warm with life.

"I almost became a forest ranger," Greg told her. "I wanted so badly to protect all the living things in the mountains when I was a kid. Once my father went deer hunting. I was so mad I didn't speak to him for a week. It was hard on me, growing up in central California where boys were expected to hunt. But after a while it looked kind of silly for anyone to call me a sissy. I was bigger than most of them and a hell of a lot tougher when I had to be.

"Over there's a hedgehog cactus. You don't want to sit down on one of those. See the cactus apples on the prickly pears? They're ruby red in daylight. The desert never lets a man starve, you just have to know what to look for. I've already taught Davy how to survive in the wilds."

"Did I tell you you're a nice man?" Leslie said, swept up into his mood of earthy reality. She found herself loving the vibration of his low, soft voice. It washed over her like a soothing balm, but it also left a ripple of sensuality in its wake.

He stopped walking and turned around to face her. "If you want a lecture, you'll have to stop distracting the tour guide. I'm doing my best not to notice how lovely you look in the moonlight. Shall we continue?"

"I'm sorry. How long is this tour, by the way?"

"Just to the bottom of the canyon and back. I'll carry you out if I have to, but I want to show you my favorite place."

She took a deep, steadying breath. "Lead the way."

"Okay. Watch your step now—we're going over a dry stream bed and the ground's uneven."

The trail became steeper and more heavily wooded. "I hear water," Leslie said.

"Mission Creek. A couple of late summer rains brought it back to life. This area is a riparian woodland. That means it's a typical river environment. White alder and bigleaf maple at the water's edge, a western sycamore or two, some black cottonwood just starting to turn yellow. But the prettiest plant of all is this one." He pointed to a shiny-leafed bush. "But if you touch it you'll break out in itchy welts all over your body."

"Poison oak?"

"Some people are even sensitive to being near it. I've never had a problem with it, though. In fact, my cabin is smack in the middle of a lot of this stuff."

They walked to the bottom of the canyon. Leslie smelled the complicated odors of the many varieties of trees and shrubs as they followed the boulder-strewn creek bed.

"You just missed the canyon sunflowers and the tiger lilies. By September their flowers are gone. Only a few poor poppies here and there." He squeezed Leslie's hand. "We're almost to my spot."

Leslie's nerves were singing with the heady potion of smells and sensations of this habitat that was truly

Greg's. A huge rock loomed up before them, as big as a house, with ferns clustered around its base and a section of its mass jutting out into the creek. Greg stopped. "Feel up to a climb? I'll help you."

Her heart turned over with a thump. She had a terrible fear of heights, and here in the bottom of the canyon even the moon was having trouble offering its light. "Your spot is up there?" she asked with a catch in her voice.

"On the very top. I promise you'll love it. Trust me. There are footholds, and I'll be right behind you."

Greg's enthusiasm gave her courage, and she put a tentative foot up to the first cleft in the boulder and reached to grab an outcropping. With his strong hand bracing her ankle she felt safe. Never in her life had she voluntarily climbed such a height. The problem would be in getting down, but Greg would be with her.

"Got it?" he called. "I'm coming up, but I'll keep a hand on you."

They scrambled the twenty feet to the top where a cool platform of rock was waiting for them.

"I come here with Davy and we sit up high and watch the birds in the trees, eye to eye. This was probably an old Chumash ceremonial rock—look at all the small round holes chiseled in it. They followed the sun and moon paths in some way we don't yet know about, but it had to do with those patterns of holes they drilled into certain special rocks." He put his arm around Leslie's shoulder and drew her against him. "End of lecture. Now tell me what you're thinking. Does any of this make sense to you?"

"I love it," she said softly, bemused by him completely.

"I love thinking about the Indian ceremonies and the creatures in the trees, and your riparian woodland," she said softly. "I feel as if I've just discovered a wonderful secret."

He brushed a kiss across her temple, very lightly. "You've never been in this kind of place before—never been camping?"

"Not even once. My father and mother weren't the outdoorsy type, except for weekend sailing once in a while on Dad's little boat."

Two owls were hooting messages to one another from across the canyon, and something scuttled over the boulder and down again. "My best friends," Greg said. "Some nights I camp here with Davy and teach him to recognize the sounds of the animals. Hear that scratching? It's a raccoon hunting under a rock for grubs." He moved until his lips grazed her cheek and the corner of her mouth. "Don't make a sound," he whispered. They kissed with only the rustling of the raccoon's busy digging breaking the silence.

How good it felt to kiss him again, Leslie thought, and then he pulled slightly back to take a deep breath. "I wanted to be sure it was as good as I remembered," he echoed her thoughts. "What do you think?"

Leslie said nothing for a moment, trying to pull out of the overwhelming mood of romance that threatened to swamp her. "Maybe we shouldn't tempt the gods," she finally replied in a small voice.

He smoothed her hair with his hand. "Is this a wrong turn we're taking, Les?"

His warmth flowed around her, and she leaned into his caress, her eyes closed. "I'm not sure."

"Every time I touch you I almost have a cardiac arrest," he admitted, his voice ragged. "Is it only me, Les, or do you feel it, too?"

From deep inside his enclosing bulk Leslie whispered, "All the more reason for us to leave this place and go home." She was shivering from the tension of needing him and trying to deny it.

"You're a woman of wisdom, Miss O'Neill," he said in a low voice.

"I know . . . dammit." She sighed, looking up at his craggy face.

His eyes glinted, he was looking at her with such intensity. "So I suppose it would be very unwise if we—" His mouth came down slowly over hers, warm and enveloping, drawing a soft groan from her throat. *Dammit*, she thought futilely as clouds of sensation moved across her rational mind, blotting out all resistance.

The kiss went on and they moved together until they were lying upon the thick mat of leaves covering the rock. Greg held her gently, as if he had something very precious in his arms. Their natural bed rustled, shaping itself to their bodies. "To hell with wisdom," he murmured against her lips.

"Mmm," she answered, reveling in the sweet abrasion of his beard against her face and throat. "Ahh," she sighed when his kiss moved along her throat.

"Ahh, yourself," he kidded huskily as one hand smoothed a pathway upward beneath her bulky sweater until it found the firm swell of her breast.

Their bodies had adjusted to each other until they fitted together like two halves of a magic puzzle, and Leslie knew she was fast losing control. A firestorm was raging inside her, whipping along her spine, robbing her of caution, beckoning her onward recklessly.

Greg's mouth discovered her sensitive earlobe, and his tongue started to trace her ear's delicate inner folds. Then he lifted himself a little away from her and, his eyes gleaming in the moonlight, searched her face for permission. In answer, she smiled and brought her sweater up over her head, making a pillow for them.

Once again their kiss was a smooth silken bridge between them. A powerful shudder went through Leslie's body and she begged, "Don't stop" as his fingertips brushed the thin lace covering her breasts. Unhooking her bra at the front, he brought his mouth down to her hard nipples, lingering over them until she was trembling uncontrollably in his arms.

Suddenly he released her and tore off his own shirt. Then he watched as she undid her jeans. He skimmed his work pants down along his legs. Their faces shone with smiles. And then, in the moonlight they began the slow ritual of lovemaking. Savoring every touch and sensation, they watched each other with joy, not wanting to close their eyes to the beauty of what they were sharing.

His gentle, eager hands traced her body as if he needed to memorize all of her. He ran a trail of kisses down across her breasts and with his tongue circled her navel. Slowly, slowly his mouth pursued its path along her soft inner thighs. She moaned with unabashed pleasure, inviting him to know her most secret places. After a long breathless moment he brought his sweet mouth back to hers for a reassuring kiss while those hands she adored gently stroked and explored. She felt the growing hardness of his sex against her body, straining to release its power.

As Greg pleasured her, so Leslie brought pleasure to him. And then, enclosing his hardness with her hands, she guided him to her, ready for him, desperate to be complete with him inside her. She felt his whole body shudder as he threw off the restraining bonds of his willpower.

"Yes!" he groaned, "Oh, yes!" He kissed her now, covering her body with the length of his to slowly enter the sanctuary of her. They were joined at last, irrevocably and with a cry of joy. A night bird called out long and high, and for an exquisite moment they didn't move, their bodies sending subtle signals of sweet ecstasy from deep within.

Then, when they could trust themselves to control the force of their mutual desire, they began the ancient rhythm of love, their bodies linked in perfect pairing. They uttered words from the depths of their beings as the rhythm of their ritual increased. Then with a primeval cry of completion, they fell silent once more, awed by the power that was theirs to invoke.

High above the leaf-strewn nest, the moon and stars moved in stately silence. And through the night the man and woman came to one another, again and again, until the morning birds were waking and a wash of color streaked the cobalt sky from the eastern horizon.

Greg had long before propped himself on one elbow to watch Leslie's slow, contented breathing. He covered her with her sweater, although there was no need, for her body still glowed with heat.

He let a shiny beetle crawl over his hand and down again and breathed deeply of the damp clean air of morning. *I don't dare call it love*, he warned himself, trying not to reach for Leslie again, to start their lovemaking anew, trying not to think that it had been eight years since he had felt like this—since Celeste had turned his life upside down. He dangled an ocher-toned sycamore leaf over Leslie's face until she opened her eyes and smiled a besotted smile.

"We might want to put some clothes on before the dear old ladies of the garden guild take their morning walk," he whispered. "And there's a squirrel who's been looking accusingly at us for a long time."

"I don't want to go," she whispered back and reached a sleepy hand up to ruffle his already disheveled hair. She didn't want to return to that other world where everything had to make sense. She shut her eyes again.

He leaned down to kiss her soft, warm lips and pulled away quickly. "The ladies will be scandalized. We can't have that." Wishing he trusted himself enough to stroke her perfect body one more time, he began to explain, "Never in my life..."

"Never in mine, either," she said, wanting him again.

"I'll never forget tonight." He cast a wry look at the brightening sky overhead. "Last night," he corrected. "I think we taught the spirits of this place a thing or two about—" He stopped short, wanting to say *love.* "About what happens when two people give a wonderful gift to each other."

They were both smiling, but as they dressed their thoughts were painful and their bodies were hungry.

7

ON THE DRIVE HOME Leslie's body was humming from the effects of their long night of lovemaking. She watched Greg as he drove, knowing that he had succeeded in wiping away all memory she had of any other man.

Her lips curved in a rueful smile. "Well, *señor*, what now?" She reached over to rest her hand on his upper thigh and he smiled.

"I don't know. Do you want to call it quits, now that we know how dangerous it is for us to be alone together?"

"No," she said with conviction. "That's the coward's way out."

"If you don't want the car to go off the road, you'd better put your delicious hand back in your provocative lap," he warned. "So you don't advise cowardice, Miss O'Neill? Why not stagger through the day doing our separate errands and have a little chat about things over supper." He turned the Jeep into the Seaview Inn's driveway, turned off the engine and let it coast down to the back garage. "Ofelia sleeps with one eye open," he explained.

They tiptoed into the house through the back door and stood at the foot of the stairs holding hands.

"Breakfast in an hour, but all I want is you." He leaned close for a kiss, but the loud clearing of a throat stopped him. Mr. Blaine was striding from the parlor with a walking stick in one hand and a book in the other.

"Ah, Mr. Austin. Good morning! And Miss O'Neill. I've been reading the most interesting work. It seems that there are over one thousand descendants of the Chumash Indian tribes still in existence in the area. Your boy seemed quite interested in the subject."

Leslie started to pull away and leave the two men together, but Greg wouldn't release her hand. He glared at her for trying to desert him. "Davy and I are real fans of the Chumash," he said. "It's good to know they aren't all gone."

"Far from it," Mr. Blaine responded earnestly. "Oh, well, I'm off for my morning constitutional. Until breakfast, then?" He set a brisk course for the front door.

Greg swept Leslie into his arms impatiently. "I wonder if Mr. Blaine ever spent the night on a boulder making love to a wild and beautiful creature like you. It might change his interests considerably."

"You're terrible! Now you'd best go wake up your son and pretend you slept here last night." She started up the stairs.

"Are you having second thoughts?" he whispered after her.

"I'm scared to death," she answered honestly.

"Me too."

THE TRAY WAS still on the floor outside her door, with the little glass emptied of its wine. It seemed a lifetime ago when she had gulped her sherry and stormed from the house, ready to mow down anyone in her path.

Even though the air in the room was cool, her body felt warm. Greg's own special kind of fire still circulated through her veins, flushing her skin with high color. She shed her sweater and bra, and thought of him. How she loved his rugged, powerful body! How she wanted to touch him and feel him respond to her. How perfect it would feel to have his essence inside her once more. She remembered too well the way his fingers and lips and tongue and taut, thrusting, muscular body had made love to her.

But suddenly, like a distant warning, a cold feeling crept over her. Perhaps she had done something she would regret. Shivering, she pulled her fragmented thoughts back to the real world of Olson and Loeb and her survey team.

"The mall," she said aloud. "Justin's new account." She made a face and dropped herself into the rocking chair. Justin's instructions in hand, she concentrated on trying to make sense of them. At first her eyes refused to focus, but after a few breaths she was better. At least she wasn't in danger of drowning in her own wild fantasies.

At breakfast Greg greeted Leslie as any good host would, but Ofelia looked ready to burst with curiosity.

"Good morning," Leslie replied. She heard the huskiness in her voice and knew that Greg was smiling inwardly at her, though his face betrayed nothing.

Davy, missing one slipper, rushed in, rubbing his eyes. "Hi, Miss O'Neill. Are you still takin' me to the zoo today?"

"Absolutely. If you can wait until three o'clock. I have to work until then." Davy's green eyes were so much like Greg's, she thought. Perceptive and innocent at once, they held wisdom behind the boyish gleam.

"Davy likes the old lion they have there," Greg said, leaning close to serve Leslie fresh orange juice, and her spine tingled with remembered excitement. He swung a long leg over his chair, dropping easily into it, and went on innocently, "Did he mention that his dad likes to see the old lion, too?"

Leslie caught Davy's conspiratorial grin. "Not a word."

"I'm just kidding," Greg said. "I can't join you, anyway. I'm spending the afternoon on a project. I have to survey a mesa back of Ventura."

Leslie watched his lips moving, hardly noticing what he said. *Don't do anything this afternoon,* she wanted to say. *Let's just be together somewhere, naked to the sky.* Greg smiled at her, and they spoke with their eyes.

Just then, Mr. Blaine walked into the kitchen. "I could smell the grand coffee a block away, Mrs. Reyes," he said enthusiastically. "It's good to be in a household where everyone is stirring at an early hour. Good morning again, Mr. Austin, Miss O'Neill."

"Top of the morning, Mr. Blaine," Greg replied, pouring him a cup of coffee. "Did you have a good walk?"

"Splendid."

Leslie stood to go and Greg followed. "I'll be right back. I need to have a word with Miss O'Neill before she leaves for the day." He took Leslie's arm and they left the room.

When they were safely out in the hall, Greg drew her hard against his chest and kissed her. "I don't know how I'm going to make it through the day, I want you so much."

She pulled away, putting a cautionary finger to his lips. "This is absolutely crazy. This is what teenagers do who've just discovered the birds and the bees."

He simply grinned, and Leslie watched him walk back into the kitchen. She felt a sense of loss when the door shut behind him.

AFTER AN HOUR spent over Justin's closely typed instructions, Leslie was beginning to feel the effects of spending the night on a hard boulder. Her back was sore when she moved a certain way and she seemed tender all over from the hours spent on her sycamore-and-oak-leaf mattress. But beyond such small discomforts she still felt Greg's skin upon hers, the texture of his fine body hairs, the wonderful hardness of his muscular torso, his slow, measured movements...

She picked up her briefcase and tape recorder. *Fools rush in...* The old phrase taunted her. If someone asked her right now what she was doing, she would have to admit she didn't know. A week ago she would have laughed at the very idea of leaping into a new love affair. Where was the reserve that she once had—the sense of self-preservation that had saved her from falling in love with Derek?

The fleeting thought of Derek reminded her of his letter and airline tickets to Europe. On her way out, she called Western Union and sent a telegram to him.

Cancel Concorde flight. If you need more explanation I'll be at Biltmore Tuesday. Sorry you don't understand.

Leslie

She owed him the courtesy of one last explanation, and then if he still refused to honor her decision, that would be his problem, not hers.

Her six teammates were waiting for her at the café where they'd arranged to meet. If anyone noticed that their leader looked exhausted and strangely distracted, no one said it.

"It's called Bon Homme," she informed them, "and it's a line of men's cosmetics and personal items designed to appeal to the new image of the American man—young, sophisticated but natural, and upwardly mobile." Leslie talked for a while, repeating Justin's words and not really thinking about them.

"Miss O'Neill?" Jan said, "I'm afraid some of the guys on the campuses will laugh at all this stuff." She was referring to the pictures of towel-wrapped male models posed with body powder, hair spray, facial astringents and wrinkle cream.

"That's what the Bon Homme people want us to find out," Leslie said.

Jan's partner, Allen, spoke up. "Maybe they'll make fun of it in public, but I'll bet they'll admit they like it if we let 'em make out the opinion forms in private. Why don't we fix up a kind of booth or something?"

Leslie was grateful for the ideas. She had enough wits left to agree to creative suggestions from the others. With good feelings and several more cups of coffee to fortify them, the team picked up their new material and set out for the day. Leslie would spend her time circulating among the three locations.

Someday she would confess to Justin that the success of this team didn't have much to do with Leslie O'Neill, but for now she was relieved to be the leader of people who were so bright and self-motivated.

At two-thirty she made her final round of the day, collecting the survey material and reminding everyone that Sunday wasn't a day of rest for them. She scheduled the locations for the next day and aimed her car toward home.

Her legs balked at the effort to climb the broad steps of the Seaview Inn's front porch. While she stood contemplating the possibility of taking a short nap on the ground before proceeding, Davy bounded out the front door and down to where Leslie was standing.

"I'm ready!" he said, his freckles and red hair seemingly in animated motion as he grinned up at her.

She drew a deep, resigned breath. "I have some old running shoes in my room. Do you think you could go up and get them for me? They're in the big wardrobe. Here, take my key."

"Sure," he said, already launching back up the steps.

Leslie sat down on the bottom step. This was asking too much of her poor body, but she couldn't disappoint Davy.

He had a brown paper bag in one hand and her shoes in the other when he returned. "Ofelia gave me some tortilla chips in case we get hungry. She wanted to talk to you, but I said you didn't have time," he told her breathlessly, urging her with his green eyes to hurry tying her shoes.

"Let's go, then." The thought of Ofelia waiting to talk helped Leslie find new strength.

The Santa Barbara Zoo was a small, friendly place set back from the beach road, not far from where last night's midnight jog had taken place. In a caged enclosure, the old lion lay chasing flies and ignoring the faces of his visitors. He seemed to have a philosophical outlook on his situation, only occasionally raising his eyes at a new noise, then returning to lick one of his huge golden paws. Davy was disappointed.

He pulled her along until they came to the monkey section. There they watched the comic behavior of the varied species of small primates. Davy laughed heartily, a high-pitched version of his father's wonderful laugh. Eventually they moved on to look at the dazzling array of tropical birds in their high enclosures.

Leslie was beginning to see double by the time they had strolled the length and breadth of the lovely little zoo. She found herself leaning against walls and railings.

"I told ya you'd like it here." Davy beamed up at her while they walked back to the parking lot.

Leslie smiled. "I loved it, especially seeing your lion."

"Next time we can get here in the morning and watch 'em eat. That's lots of fun."

A lump formed in her throat. "Davy. . . I'll be leaving Santa Barbara next week. Maybe I can come up again . . . sometime."

"Sure you can. My dad said he's gonna take you to see the Indian caves."

"He did?"

"Yep." He slipped a thin hand into hers as they neared the car. "I told him it was okay with me. We can go after we get back from Phila . . . Phila . . . I don't know how to say it."

"Philadelphia," she whispered and tried not to show her concern. All at once she felt selfish, reminded that there was pain so close to her and she had been blissfully ignoring it. "Maybe when you get back from Philadelphia, we'll see the caves together." She patted his warm, ruddy cheek.

"Ya want an ice-cream cone?" he offered eagerly. "I've got some money left from my allowance."

"You're on," she replied, laughing, and they got into the car. Following Davy's directions, she drove back up State Street.

"What do you want to do when you grow up?" she asked. They were sitting on the curb slowly eating double-decker cones.

He shrugged. "I want to be with my dad. I'll learn all about rocks and stuff, maybe have a place to help sick animals—I dunno."

"I'll bet you'd be terrific with the animals."

"Ofelia won't let me have a snake or anything, but when I get bigger I'm gonna build a place for some turtles and rabbits."

"I had a rabbit when I was a girl. Her name was Bessie."

Davy stopped licking his ice cream for a moment. "Do you live very far away?"

"Los Angeles. That's about two hours. Not far."

"Can you write it down for me? So I can send you a letter?"

"Your dad has my address in the register, but if you want one for yourself, I'll write it for you." There was something so earnest in his eyes as he asked her. She reached into her purse for a notepad and pen and carefully printed her name and address.

"Thanks," he said. "I'm a good printer, you know?"

"I'd love you to write me a letter, Davy," she said and ran her hand through his wayward red hair.

When they arrived back at the inn Davy hugged her around the waist and dashed off. She urged her feet up the stairs and along the hall. The image of her soft canopied bed beckoned to her, and when she had kicked off her shoes and flopped back onto the bright patchwork quilt, she let out a long sigh. Her thoughts were fragmented; nothing seemed connected with anything else. There was too much to sort out about last night. Today was something she had gotten through by willpower alone, and though Derek's crumpled letter was gone she still had to face him once more. She turned her head into the soft down pillow and shut out everyone.

GREG WAS EXHAUSTED when he came down from Piggott's Mesa. He'd been surveying a large parcel of land for a man who wanted to divide it into five-acre residential lots. The job involved finding future erosion patterns and possible slippage in case of earthquake. Greg used conventional tools of analysis, but the owner also wanted him to locate spring water, and for that Greg used a very old and unconventional method. His best success in finding underground water had always been with dowsing.

He stowed his favorite willow branch beneath the seat of the Jeep, smiling wryly. Arnold Murchison need never know that the high-priced geologist located his precious water with a divining rod. He looked up at the afternoon sky and saw a California condor in the distance near Topa Topa Ridge, slowly coasting on an updraft. Not many of the birds were left anymore. The mavericks of the earth always have trouble, he thought.

Greg Austin knew enough about human psychology to realize what he had done last night with the lovely Leslie. He had played Adam and Eve with her, pretending that nothing else existed, and now he was scared—scared to see her again for fear the illusion would have vanished. There she would be, just a nice lady who had joined him in his idiot fantasy for a night. What if everything looked different the next time he saw her? Then what was he going to do—apologize and say he didn't mean any harm?

He kicked at the stony earth with his boot. *Great guy,* he growled inwardly. The keen awareness of her had haunted him all day, making his body restless with desire while his mind made it impossible for him to enjoy the feeling.

Where could they go after last night? Free love on a bed of leaves under the full moon was the limit of most people's erotic imaginations. Never mind the afterglow that was there this morning—his gut feeling was that the spell would be broken when he saw her again.

Greg jammed the Jeep into low gear and started the slow, rocky descent to Old Foothill Road. By now Leslie was probably thinking what a big mistake it all was, he brooded. But then he remembered how she had held him and brought him to those incredible heights and he couldn't believe that she had been at all unwilling. In fact, maybe she had seduced him. Maybe he'd better start running fast the other way. The chemistry was too volatile, more than he could handle right now.

He laughed out loud at himself. *You self-destructive SOB. Nearly talked yourself all the way around and out the other side.* Just because Celeste had run over him with a Mack truck and left him by the side of the road was no reason to back off at the first sign of something great.

Seeing Leslie's car in the driveway, he felt his heart start to race. He looked up to the second floor, to her room; there was no light. Where was she?

Ofelia met him at the back door as he was juggling his maps. He'd been hoping to disappear silently into his office.

"Davy had a good time at the zoo," she said cheerfully. "Miss O'Neill is in her room with a Do Not Disturb sign on her door. Is she well?" Ofelia looked hopefully into his face, watching for reaction.

He shrugged, but his stomach was in a knot. "You know as much as I do."

She untied her big flowered apron and folded it carefully. "Well, I hope there is no problem. My father waits for me and I must go now."

"Give him my best," Greg told her kindly.

"I leave lots of food in the kitchen for dinner. Do not forget the new guests, *señor*. Everything is okay in the big bedroom for when they come." She picked up her plastic tote bag and walked past Greg. "You be good to Miss O'Neill," she added. "She look tired to me."

"Fine, Ofelia," Greg assured her, wishing she would go. "See you in the morning. Oh, where's Davy?"

"He spend the night with Mike next door. I talked to the mother. Have a happy evening," she said meaningfully and pulled the back door shut behind her.

The house was still. Greg went to the kitchen desk and looked at the register. Mr. Blaine had checked out at noon and the newlywed Silverwoods were due to arrive any minute. He set down his work materials, deciding to make sure that the Victorian double bed in the large south room was properly made up and that the champagne and glasses were ready in the ice bucket.

The Do Not Disturb sign on Leslie's door jumped out at him. He wished he knew what state of mind she was in.

LESLIE STIRRED from her nap at the sound of footsteps and voices in the hallway outside. The door next to her room opened and closed and a woman's voice spoke excitedly in counterpoint to a man's. New guests, Leslie's sleep-drugged brain registered. She wondered what time it was and looked over at the travel clock. Not quite seven. She closed her eyes.

After a while she woke again. The couple were laughing delightedly and a loud pop came from their room. Champagne.

Leslie got up and paced, then changed into a comfortable lavender silk jump suit and brushed her hair. Greg must have forgotten that they had a date for dinner. He should have contacted her by now, she reasoned.

A shiver rushed through her at the thought of seeing him again. She walked to the end of the hall and looked out the window to the side garden. The Jeep was in the garage. She felt her heart constrict painfully; he was home.

Still barefoot, she walked down the stairs, alert for signs of him. His office door was closed. As she stood indecisively, feeling suddenly shy, the door opened and Greg was there.

"Hi," she said, her voice barely audible.

"Hi. How was your day? Ofelia was worried about your Do Not Disturb sign." He looked almost stern.

"I was taking a nap after work. How... how was your day?"

"Okay." They stood looking at each other for an uncomfortable moment until Greg said softly, "I missed you, Les. I really did." His guarded expression eased, to be replaced by a lopsided smile. "I tried not to, but I did."

"I missed you, too," she whispered.

They didn't move toward each other. The grandfather clock struck seven.

"It's seven o'clock," she pointed out unnecessarily.

"Seems to be. How do you feel?"

"Awkward—" she smiled "—and sore."

"Me too. My back aches... and a few other unmentionable places." He grinned back at her. "Hungry?"

"I can't tell."

He put out a hand to take hers. "How about some leftovers?"

"Fine." Her voice caught in her throat, and his hand closed tighter around hers.

"You're shaking."

"I know." Tears started to bank against her lower lids.

"Oh, Les..." He pulled her to him and held her tightly against his chest. They stood wrapped in each other's arms for a long time, rocking slowly, saying nothing. He brushed his lips across the crown of her head. "We've started something, haven't we?" he said at last.

"I'm afraid so," she admitted, her face against his warm broad chest.

THEY SAT at the round kitchen table picking at their cold enchiladas and rice, neither one daring to expand on the subject occupying both their minds. "I wasn't great company for your son today," she confessed. "He had to drag the old woman all over the zoo."

"I'll bet he loved it. You're the first female friend of mine to be so honored. He thinks my taste is rotten."

Leslie looked at his boyish face and smiled. "I think I did an adequate job with my team today, but I'm not sure. I was half asleep."

"What do you say to something more conservative tonight—like the master's quarters in the old tower? Davy's spending the night with the neighbors. Ofelia's out, too. That leaves us and the honeymoon couple." He took her hand across the table and kissed her palm lightly, sending a ripple of pleasure along her spine. "What about it? No more boulders."

She hesitated. "Boulders aren't the problem."

"It doesn't have to be like last night," he said, sorry he had gone too fast. "I just want to be with you. I want you to fall asleep in my arms, that's all."

"I feel very strange. A little like a cyclone just went through my house, and I haven't assessed the damage yet."

"And you're going back to L.A. in a few days," he said slowly. "Do you want to call it off right now and let it go at that? I didn't want to do any damage, Les. But I can't pretend nothing happened between us."

She dredged up a smile in response to his understatement.

"Well," he challenged quietly, "does that kind of thing happen to you every day? It sure as hell doesn't to me."

She met his gaze. "We did it all backward—that's what bothers me. I don't know if it's possible to start over and do it the right way."

"I can't erase last night, Les."

"I know," she whispered. "I haven't been on a lot of boulders in my life. I mean, there haven't been a lot of men . . ."

"Oh?" he arched an eyebrow.

"Don't make fun of me. I have to say this."

"It's none of my business. You told me that yourself."

She ignored him and went on. "With Derek it was a gradual thing. I didn't start out wanting to have an affair with him. I certainly didn't jump into his bed the first time he beckoned."

"I'd just as soon not hear about it," Greg protested.

"We dated for a long time before... When I first came to Los Angeles I didn't know anybody and he was good company. Then after a time he thought I'd make a perfect mate to fit in with his life-style. I never loved him," she finished quietly.

"Poor old Derek." His voice was almost sympathetic.

"I'm seeing him Tuesday night to settle things once and for all, and I'm not looking forward to it. Things were finished between us before I came to Santa Barbara. Derek just refused to—"

"Miss O'Neill," he interrupted. "It's time you got some sleep. We're both too tired for a conversation like this. I think you should at least see the tower room, then make up your mind where you want to spend the night. No pressure, no wild scenes. I'm bone tired, too."

She nodded and stretched out her hand toward him.

Greg led her up the spiral staircase to the tower. On the second floor was Davy's room, a small curved space that followed the shape of the stairwell. The third floor was Greg's private domain—a round room with high narrow windows and a 360-degree view of the world. There were no curtains, and the only furniture was a simple pine wardrobe and a platform on which was spread a thick muslin sleeping pad. The fragrant smell of fresh pine filled the stark room.

"Well, what do you think?" he asked.

"I feel like I'm up in a forest ranger station."

He laughed and brought her to the low bed. "The bed sack's filled with pine needles I brought from my cabin, along with some fresh rosemary. The pillows, too."

Leslie pressed down on the mattress; it made a soft rustling noise. "Doesn't it prickle?"

"Nope. It's what our ancestors used. The muslin's dense, and I sleep like a baby. You will, too."

"And the rosemary keeps away the evil spirits?"

"You're learning. What do you think? Want to give it a try here tonight, or would you still rather be alone?"

She smiled back at him. "I want to be here."

"Then why don't you go back to your room and get ready for bed and meet me up here? I assure you I'll be appropriately attired."

Ten minutes later, she knocked at the tower door and was met by Greg wearing paisley pajama bottoms, a robe and slippers. "Don't laugh," he ordered. "I keep these for formal occasions. Come in."

Greg turned down the heavy comforter and patted the pillows. "My lady—" he bowed "—choose your side."

Leslie started to chuckle. "Where did you get that outfit?"

"It's not important. Just come to bed, woman. I can't wait to have my arms around you." He switched off the light.

Leslie slipped out of her robe and into the bed; the bed sack rustled under her weight. In the semidarkness she felt Greg's body next to hers and then his strong arms wrapped around her until her face rested against his chest. "Is that what starting at the beginning feels like? It's a hell of a good feeling." His voice was thick with fatigue.

"Good night, dear friend," she whispered.

He raised his head a little in protest. "Is that all I am?"

"That's what's best for us tonight."

"Woman's wisdom again," he mumbled. His breath moved into a heavy, peaceful rhythm and he was asleep.

Leslie smiled and snuggled her cheek against the fine hairs of his chest. The sound of his strong heartbeat was pure pleasure.

8

LESLIE AWOKE to the smell of pine all around her. She stirred slightly beneath the comforter and opened her eyes, feeling like a hibernating bear just waking from a winter's sleep. Greg was standing over her, half-naked and smiling.

"I want to show you something," he said softly. "I've been waiting for a sign of life."

She stretched her arms above her head and yawned, thinking how perfectly natural it felt to have this blond god smiling down at her. "What do you want to show me?"

"You'll have to come out of your cocoon to see it."

He led her to one of the high windows of the tower room where the view stretched endlessly over the Pacific Ocean. "The islands," he said, pointing toward them. "The winds changed in the night." He put an arm around her waist and they stood for a long time drinking in the beauty of the view.

"It's an optical illusion," Leslie murmured. She felt she could reach out and touch the craggy cliffs and jutting peninsulas below them. "They look so wild and untouched."

"The long one on the left is Santa Cruz Island. Santa Rosa's next to it, then San Miguel. I've walked all over them at one time or another. They rarely offer strangers a sight like this one. Usually you have to come to them."

"They're fantastic."

"I thought you'd appreciate them." He slipped his arm around her waist and they embraced easily. "I heard Ofelia come in a few minutes ago. She'll be starting breakfast."

"Bed and breakfast," Leslie said. "It never occurred to me what that could mean." She stood on her toes to kiss his lips.

"Uh-oh," he whispered and pulled her closer. "Feel what you do to me. On Sunday mornings my folks always locked their bedroom door. Maybe we should, too." His eyes flickered with a sensual light.

Leslie felt her own desire kindling with the pressure of Greg's taut body against hers. "Just look at me," she breathed shakily, "I'm as weak as a kitten. I'm not sure I like being so—" Her words were smothered by Greg's warm lips.

"Less talk," he whispered, brushing the lightest of kisses against her eyelids and then down again to her welcoming lips.

"Mmm," she agreed, loving the strength that she drew from his powerful body, amazed that such feelings could possibly exist. There was no hurry, no awareness of time as they entered their kingdom of delights and pulled the magic cloak around themselves once more, making the rest of the world vanish until they bade it return again. The sun's light moved slowly across the room.

With their passion spent, they lay together for a long time. Neither wanted to move, to make separate what had been joined in such joy. At length, Greg's hand stroked her damp hair from her face and she felt his body move from hers, heard his deep sigh of contentment.

"Greg?" she whispered in a low, husky voice, not wanting to open her eyes yet. "What do you think this wild thing is?"

He was quiet for a moment, then his hand reached over to take hers. "Damned if I know. Some kind of tornado, maybe."

She heard the smile in his voice, but still she didn't want to open her eyes. "I'm serious. If we keep on doing this, what will we have to say to each other—you're great in bed? I mean...is this all we have, or is it more?" She opened her eyes to see him looking over at her, very seriously this time.

He brought her hand to his lips. "You're right, of course. I'm like a drunken sailor on a binge. I can't get enough of you. I want to carry you off to the hills and never let you go home again."

He released her hand and left the bed to stand at one of the high windows. The sunlight was a golden glow around him, and he looked so beautiful that she couldn't continue to speak.

Turning to look at her, he said, "I have to take a step back, don't I? Otherwise we'll never know..."

She came up behind him and slipped her arms around his waist. "I don't want to wake up some morning with regrets. I've done that already, and I don't like the feeling."

He smiled indulgently. "If you're going to tell me about any more men, don't. I could probably reel off a few case histories that would make me sound like the last man on earth you want to be tied up with. You don't know me, lady."

"You can't be all bad," she said. "Ofelia likes you, and Davy worships you."

"I shouldn't kid about these things, Les, but right now I don't trust my judgment any more than I'd trust a rattler not to strike if I stepped on him. There are a lot of things in life I don't trust. I never seem to know when something is going to cut me down." His voice had changed until it was dark and heavy.

Leslie had a sudden, awful thought. "Do you trust me, Greg?"

He didn't answer right away. "Maybe I don't trust life," he said, as if to himself.

She had a vision of the dark-haired Celeste in the photo, and the handsome, smiling husband at her side. "Are you still in love with your wife?" Her pulse was racing now.

"That's a crazy question," he shot back. "Why did you ask that?"

"Because I don't want to be a substitute for something you lost," she answered honestly.

There was silence between them. Greg let out his breath slowly. "Celeste is dead. Our relationship was dead long before that car crash."

"And how long was it before you could really trust a woman again?"

"Still taking surveys?" he inquired with an edge to his voice. Separating himself from her, he reached for his bathrobe, his stance truculent. "Don't try amateur psychology on me. I've had more than my share of that, Miss O'Neill."

"And I don't need to be told I'm interfering, when all I want is to make some sense out of things." She was almost shouting and felt wretchedly isolated from his comfort. "You don't know me, either. I'm not just a sexy little thing, good for a few nights. For your information, I loved last night. I loved being close to you and holding you. It was so much more than sex—it was real! Don't judge me by women you've known. It isn't fair."

The atmosphere in the tower room was thick with gathering anger. After an interminable silence, Greg spoke again. "All right, what are your terms?"

She started to laugh—he sounded so much like a capitulating general. "You mean you still want to make something out of this insanity we've started?"

"If you do, yes," he said. "And I don't tolerate laughter in my own room." He turned around and she saw that he was smiling at her again.

"Let's give ourselves some space for a while, Greg, even for a couple of days. Nothing too intense . . ."

He reached out a hand toward her. "Agreed. And we'll talk, lots of talk, to take my mind off more delightful things."

"We'll talk." She smiled and shook his hand to close the deal.

Greg watched her go and heard her bare footfalls on the tower staircase. He wondered how such a small, beautiful nymph could know so much about handling him. He wasn't sure he completely liked that.

LESLIE DRESSED halfheartedly for the day, unable to think of anything but her stupidity. She'd been wrong to fall into Greg's arms so fast, wrong to expect him to pull back at her command. She hadn't the slightest idea what she wanted from their relationship. Excitement? No. She stopped herself. That wasn't it at all. She wanted to be with Greg more than she had ever wanted anything before. How much space did they need, she wondered. How much could she bear?

There was a light knock at her door. "*¿Señorita?* I have a tray for you."

Leslie opened the door to Ofelia and a tray of steaming, fragrant food. "How sweet of you," she said, not at all hungry.

"Señor Austin say you maybe like this in your room. He is gone out early. I don't like it when he forget to eat, but he is a man, and what do we know about men's ways?" She looked resigned to the mysteries of willful masculinity. "You feeling better today?"

She cast a quick glance around the room. Leslie was sure Ofelia knew she hadn't slept here, even though the bed was rumpled from yesterday afternoon's short nap. "I'm fine. I just needed some rest. And thanks for the tray."

"Sure. I leave the honeymoon couple a big tray, but they do not open the door. Nobody is hungry in this house today." She set the tray down on the bedside table and gave Leslie a motherly smile. "Honeymoon is a good time, *sí*?"

"I'm sure it is," Leslie agreed with an indulgent smile. "If you see Mr. Austin today, tell him thanks for sending you here with the tray."

Ofelia wrung her hands with her large brightly colored apron. "I want him to be happy again, you know?"

"I know. And thanks for everything."

For the next few hours Leslie sat on the bed with her typewriter on her lap and transcribed the Bon Homme responses and her notes on the original survey topics. To the drone of voices on the cassette tapes, her fingers moved automatically on the keyboard. Her mind was tuned to another kind of reality—the bittersweet connection that vibrated between herself and Greg.

He was right, of course. Everything was going too fast. She could check out of the Seaview and make it easier for both of them. The thought was shouted down by her determination to stay right where she was. There was magic in this place and in what was happening with Greg. This wasn't a wild fling that had to end in disaster.

Davy's voice penetrated her preoccupation. "Phone call," he piped, and his footsteps thumped away down the hall.

Leslie went downstairs and picked up the parlor phone. "Leslie? It's Justin. How are you?" His soft, well-modulated voice was a welcome sound.

"Fine. I got your packet and the Bon Homme survey is going well. Thanks for being the go-between with Derek. I'm sorry—"

"He's persistent, I'll say that for him. You aren't really taking off for a prehoneymoon trip next week, are you?" There was disapproval in his tone.

"No, Justin, that was Derek's idea, not mine."

"Of course I couldn't tell the poor fellow no. I don't run your life. But in all confidence, Leslie, this isn't a good time for you to leave work. I can't tell you more, but you're being considered for something rather special in the way of a promotion."

"Justin...you can't leave me hanging like this. What is it?"

"Can't say more. But it's a plum. So you like old Santa Barbara? I thought you would."

"Is that why you called—to dangle some bait in front of me?"

"Think of me as your Dutch uncle. I was just a little worried about your state of mind when you left Los Angeles. Thought you might want help making some important decisions...that sort of thing."

"I'm not going to Italy next week, or any other week. And you're a dear for caring so much. I just wish I had your calm approach to life." She knew he'd be smiling his worldly smile.

"I was thinking of getting you a complete set of Bach's Brandenburg Concertos for Christmas. It's fine medicine for the soul. Anything else I should know about the survey before I ring off?"

"Your team is first-rate. The survey almost runs it-self. I'll have a fat portfolio for your desk when I get back."

"Excellent," the mellow voice intoned.

"See you next week."

A plum, Leslie pondered, setting down the phone. She couldn't muster the proper excitement. A promotion seemed so . . . dry, even threatening. Olson and Loeb had offices all over the western United States, as far away as Colorado; she'd be lost there.

She sat on the chintz-covered window seat and looked abstractedly at the beautiful view across the trees and rooftops of the city. Even without Greg in it, Santa Barbara was becoming her town.

A black Porsche turned into the driveway and a short, casually dressed man stepped out. She watched him come to the door and ring the bell.

Ofelia burst out of the front door with a big smile on her face. After a hearty embrace, the two people talked in rapid Spanish for a while, then the man handed her a manila envelope, hugged her again and left.

Ofelia came into the parlor. "Señor Vargas," she explained. "He leaves some things for Señor Austin. Papers for Philadelphia."

"That was Mr. Austin's lawyer?"

"*Sí*. He tell me to feed him and make him in his best mood for the courtroom. I tell him okay."

"He sounds like a good friend."

"They are like brothers, but Señor Austin don't take good advice. He has too much temper, too much anger for himself."

"Does Mr. Vargas think the court case will go in Greg's favor?"

Ofelia crossed herself. "He prays, like I do. I don't want him to be hurt more, you know?"

"I know," Leslie said. "I don't want him to be hurt, either."

Ofelia reached out to take her hand. "You are the best woman to come here, *señorita*, but be careful with him. He looks like a big man, but inside he is not sure what he is doing."

"He has a better philosophy of life than most men," Leslie countered gently. "He seems to know exactly where he stands with nature, with his work. . . ."

"But not with his heart," she said emphatically. "The women come and go. And then he have times when he only want to be alone in his cabin. It is not normal for a man, I say. Even Davy get lonely when Señor Austin is like that."

"Maybe he hasn't gotten over whatever happened with his wife," she ventured, hoping Ofelia would tell her more.

"I see what is the problem. It is anger that he had such big weakness for a beautiful woman one time, and he had no control. Every man want control. I know this. He say, better to have no love, and then he play around with the women. But that is not for him. I know this." Her face was pained.

"Maybe that's exactly what he wants, at least for now."

She planted her fists firmly on her broad hips. "He sit up on his mountain every time a woman is too close. I know how he is."

"He told me he does his best thinking in his cabin."

The luminous black eyes of the Mexican woman looked dubious. "Too much thinking is no good."

Leslie smiled and didn't reply.

"You come to dinner tonight, okay? I got swordfish at the market—fresh today."

"Thanks, but I'm having dinner with some people I work with," she lied.

"Maybe tomorrow night?" she asked pointedly.

"Thanks." Leslie left the parlor feeling ungrateful. She wished she could have said something to relieve Ofelia's worries, but what could she possibly say? Greg was a lucky man to have such devoted friends around him.

She let herself out the front door and walked in the rose garden, pausing to inhale the fragrance of an especially lovely shell-pink flower. A small metal tag was twisted around the base of the plant, revealing its name—Love's Delight. The delicate honeyed rose was almost transparent, but its odor dominated the other fragrances in the little garden.

Birds chirped and dived to the ground from the old trees overhead. Leslie's attention was caught by another sound coming from inside the white-latticed gazebo a few steps away.

"Davy?" she called. No answer. "Is that you?" She walked to the gazebo where she saw the slumped figure of the red-haired boy. "Is anything the matter?"

Unhappy green eyes slowly met hers. "Nope."

"Is it all right if I come in, then? I was just enjoying your garden." He didn't say anything, and Leslie sat down beside him on the wooden bench that followed the inside shape of the hexagonal garden house. They sat together for several minutes while Leslie tried to remember what she knew of child psychology.

"I'm waitin' for my dad," he said at last. "He must've forgot he was gonna take me someplace." Disappointment shrouded him like a cloud. "But Dad never forgets."

"I'm sorry." Leslie put her arm around his shoulders and eased his rigid little body against hers. "Where was he going to take you? Maybe I can take you there instead."

He cast a sidelong look at her that said she was a poor substitute. "We were gonna get acorns up at the big gardens."

"That sounds like fun. What do you do with the acorns after that?"

"We take a special rock and crack 'em. That gets the shells off. Then we put 'em in a bag and let the creek water run over it."

"Like the Chumash did?" she guessed, hoping she didn't sound ignorant to this seven-year-old.

"Yeah. Then we come back the next day and get the bag and grind the stuff and eat it."

"But why do you put it in the water first?"

He was looking at her now, the teacher instructing his pupil. "To get the bad stuff off, of course. You can't eat acorns raw." He made a face. "Dad and me tried it once. It was awful."

"Well?" Leslie stood up. "What are we waiting for? You get the bag and I'll get my old clothes on. Okay?"

Davy ran from the gazebo toward the house and slammed the back door behind him. Leslie went up to her room, slipped out of her jump suit and pulled on an oversize plaid cotton shirt and her jeans. Acorn gathering on an autumn day sounded delightful. Going to the Botanic Gardens again was something her restless body wanted very much to do, as well. This wasn't entirely a mission of compassion for a little boy.

They drove the ten-minute route into the wild and rustic rolling hills. The air carried a scent vividly familiar to her senses. "That's sage," she told Davy.

"White sage," he corrected. "There's all different kinds."

Leslie followed Davy's rapid footsteps along the upper trail and down into the canyon bottom. In the daylight some of the romance was lost, but not quite all. She still heard the rustling of the animals, the flutters in the oaks and sycamores. Davy reached for her hand and led her off the trail to walk closer to the creek.

There were a few strollers here and there along the paths. Nobody was near the stream bed as she and Davy began climbing over and around the hundreds of small boulders on either shore where old gnarled oak trees bent over the water.

"We aren't supposed to take stuff out of here," he whispered above the pleasant rushing sound of the water. "But Dad says it's okay to get my acorns, 'cause it's for school. He got permission. I'm gonna show my class how the Indians made food."

Leslie looked at her feet, where countless acorns were strewn. "I'm sure nobody will miss a few." She picked several handfuls of the smooth acorns, some with their brown caps still in place, and dropped them into Davy's gunnysack. When they had gathered several pounds, they stopped. "What now? Where do you plan to shell them?"

"Over here," Davy said, swinging his sack over his shoulder and trotting along the stream until he disappeared around a bend.

Leslie caught up with him and her heart turned over with a thud. Davy was scampering like a monkey up the side of an enormous white boulder—*the* boulder! She stood transfixed for a moment.

"C'mon up," Davy called to her. "It's great up here. Nice and flat."

Leslie hesitated. "I can't. I'm afraid of heights."

Davy peered down at her from the high place she knew only too well. "Honest? Cantcha close your eyes, or something?"

"I'm sorry, Davy. If you'll throw down the bag with some of the acorns I'll crack them here, closer to the ground." Her nerves were humming. The boulder seemed alive, reminding her of the feeling of belonging that was hers for one unbelievable night. The half-empty sack whizzed to the ground at her feet.

"Find a good rock like this." Davy waved his own grinding stone in the air. "Hit the acorns, but not too hard. You want me to show you?"

"I think I can do it all right." She carried the sack to a flat pan-shaped rock at the water's edge and found a stone that fitted well into her hand. As she knelt so close to the looming boulder, surrounded by natural smells and sounds, she felt comfortable. It didn't matter that her knees were wet and her black hair had escaped its combs and was hanging free and unkempt.

It took ages to crack and peel the slippery acorns. In the process her hands were hit as often as the targets were, and she managed to chip several of her best fingernails. But it felt strangely good, anyway.

"I'm done," she called up to Davy, rinsing her red hands in the cool running creek water. "What do we do now?"

"I need the sack to put my stuff in."

"Here it comes." She stood up and lobbed it high into the air. *Good shot*, she congratulated herself as she began to hunt for her two lost hair combs among the shards of acorn shells around her.

Davy descended from the great rock in three bounds. "Now we gotta put it in the water," he said breathlessly.

"Have you done this before?"

"Not ezzackly," he hedged. "Dad was gonna show me, but I can do it." He fumbled with his sack and its pithy contents, trying to tie a big knot. Then he scooped a hole in the muddy earth at the edge of the creek and dropped the sack into it. But as they watched, the current started to tug the sack downstream.

"I have an idea," Leslie said. She searched around for a stick and returned to the shore. Quickly she made a new knot, tying the bag around the rough stick, which she jammed deep into the wet ground at an angle, so that part of it was firmly anchored in dry soil at the base of the boulder.

They watched as the water carried the bulky sack a little distance and stopped.

The sack bobbed a little, but it held its own against the current. "Wow," Davy breathed, "it worked." He looked at Leslie with renewed respect.

"I think it'll still be here when we come back," she replied.

"Just so we get it by Tuesday. 'Cause Wednesday's show-and-tell day. I'm gonna show my class how to make Indian food. The kids don't believe me when I tell 'em I can do it. 'Specially Roger Cranston. He says my dad makes acorn food and I just pretend I do it."

With a last look to reassure themselves that their sack was secure and well hidden from general view, they left the area. On the drive home, Leslie wondered what hand of fate had drawn her back to this place of nature spirits and secret feelings, as if to show her something about herself.

Just being here made her wish she knew the names of the birds and trees and stones, and the many pungent odors of the sage family. She didn't want to be a stranger any longer. This was Greg's world—his and Davy's. Everywhere she looked things spoke to her silently. There were special connections and ways of seeing she had yet to learn.

Davy smiled at her and put his small warm hand into hers as she drove. "You'd make a good Indian," he assured her. "I'll tell my dad."

9

LESLIE DROPPED DAVY OFF at the inn and drove up the coast several miles, enjoying the changing lights of late afternoon. Jan and Allen were supposed to be working this afternoon in the student apartment community next to the University of California campus; she turned the Mustang into the main shopping area, looking for them. The two young people were the only ones she worried about for this survey.

"You won't believe this," Jan said in a high excited voice. "We've rigged up a couple of booths for people to fill out their questionnaires and we're getting fabulous responses about Bon Homme. Really personal things." She drew Leslie aside for more privacy. "I've been thinking that opinion research would be a terrific career for me. It's great getting inside people's heads, you know what I mean?"

Leslie nodded. "It can be very satisfying, but it takes a lot of drudgery before the bosses trust you enough to let you have your own projects. Believe me, I'm a perfect example."

Jan took her arm. "Is that dinner invitation still on? Because I'd love to talk to you about everything."

"Sure." Leslie looked down at her casual clothes. "I suppose there's a place we could go around here that isn't dressy."

Leslie tried to be a good listener as they sat together in a colorful little restaurant just off campus, but her heart wasn't in it. Jan seemed pleased, anyway, just to be able to talk about herself and her future. "You've been a real help," she said as they split the check and said good-night. "I'll be sorry when the survey is over after Tuesday. Maybe you need someone to help you evaluate the material. I'm available all next week, as long as you're here."

"My boss expects to see my fine hand on everything, but thanks just the same. My last two or three days here are going to be spent holed up in my lovely Victorian room with a typewriter glued to my lap."

"Well, keep me in mind for anything you do in the future," she said hopefully.

"You're doing a good job, Jan. I mean it. I'll tell Mr. Reiner that in my report. Don't worry, I'm sure he'll have other jobs for you." She smiled at Jan's raw enthusiasm and wished she had a little more of it herself right now.

EVEN BEFORE SHE DROVE into the gravel driveway of the inn she knew Greg wasn't home. She quietly entered the big downstairs hall and climbed the steps. Just behind her, laughing and out of breath, the newlywed couple called out a cheery greeting. "We're the Silverwoods," the bride announced. "Hello, neighbor!"

Leslie found herself walking the length of the upstairs hall with them. "Are you enjoying Santa Barbara?" she asked politely.

"Incredible," the man enthused. "Have you tried dinner at El Encanto yet? The best French chef and the best wine list. Absolutely first cabin."

He reminded Leslie of Derek—the hint of snobbery, the well-tailored suit, the confidence. "Sounds nice." She smiled as she let herself into her room and said good-night. A wrapped mint was sitting in the middle of her pillow, the covers were carefully turned down and a single glass of sherry was waiting on her bedside table.

She worked until midnight, then tried to sleep but couldn't. She hadn't heard the Jeep come in yet. The Silverwoods were celebrating their new state of bliss with silly sounds and giggles. Leslie felt like an old maid casting aspersions on others' pleasure when she secretly envied them their happiness, their certainty of each other and of the future.

She wondered where she would be a week from now. Getting ready to move to some far outpost of the Olson and Loeb empire? Denver, maybe, or Phoenix? She felt very foolish resisting the idea of a promotion—the most promising thing in her short career—just to chase after a dream. How could she risk losing everything that mattered to her future?

Because, her stubborn emotions replied, *just because . . .*

Sometime in the middle of the night, as she drifted in and out of sleep, she became aware of the familiar sound of Greg's car as it slid to a stop at the side of the house. Then the distant footfalls and, finally, the shutting of doors. At last the house felt complete and she relaxed enough to fall deeply into sleep.

The alarm didn't ring at seven o'clock the next morning as it was set to do. A line of sunlight from the corner window inched its way across her bed until it bathed Leslie's face in warmth and she finally opened her eyes.

At the same moment there was a knock at the door, and Greg's voice was announcing breakfast.

She groaned. "I overslept. I won't be able to make it on time."

He knocked again. "That's why I brought you a tray. Are you going to let me in, or do I have to use my own key?"

"Give me a sec," she said, whipping off the covers and running her fingers quickly through her scrambled hair. She dived into her pink robe and spent two seconds jamming her toothbrush into her mouth for a fresh taste. When she opened the door she looked more composed than she felt.

"Well," Greg breathed. "You manage to give me pleasure just by standing there. What do you think that means?" He entered carrying a large breakfast tray laden with pretty flowered china, a bud vase with a single yellow rose and a covered silver dish.

Leslie smiled warily at this gift, then at him. "How do I rate such a fancy tray?"

"The Silverwoods are sleeping late this morning, so you get the special honeymooners' breakfast." He set his burden down on the bedside table. "As you can see, I'm obeying your wishes and keeping my distance."

He stood watching as she perched on the edge of the bed and smelled the sweet yellow rose. "As I recall," Leslie reminded him, "the desire for distance was mutual."

"I nearly brought Davy with me this morning, just to show you how honorable my intentions were, but he couldn't see why it took two people just to deliver one tray."

"Did he tell you about yesterday?"

"Oh, yes. I thought it was next Sunday we were supposed to get his acorns. I feel rotten about it. Poor Davy's been getting the short end of things lately, just when I should be spending more time with him, not less."

"Are you blaming me for that?" Leslie said, sensitive to the way Greg could suddenly switch moods, and not wanting to get caught in the transition.

He put up a hand. "No more psychology, please. I come in peace."

Leslie relented. "Davy tells me I'd make a good Indian. You know where he cracked his acorns, don't you?"

A slow grin spread across his face. "I can guess. Our boulder."

"That wasn't fair. It brought back all sorts of memories."

"So you haven't forgotten?"

She dropped her eyes from his intent green gaze. "It's not the sort of night one forgets easily," she said softly and started to pour herself a cup of tea from the little china pot.

"That's what I thought about when I was up in the cabin. And a lot of other things, like my nonexistent bank balance, my mortgage, the upcoming court appearance...and why a certain lovely black-haired woman decided to arrive on my doorstep right in the middle of all this mess. That's not exactly a smooth compliment, is it, Miss O'Neill?" he said, grimacing. "I'm having a hard time with it all, believe me."

"I have enough doubts for both of us, Greg," she said ruefully. "My life isn't exactly smooth and simple, either."

"Don't pay any attention to my griping. Now it's time to lift that little silver dome on your tray and see what your main dish is."

Suspiciously she looked at him and removed the cover from the silver dish. A white envelope rested in the middle of it. Greg was silent as she picked it up and read the handwritten invitation inside.

Mr. Gregory Austin
requests the pleasure of your company
this evening at eight o'clock

dinner/dancing

clothing required

"A date?"

"A genuine, honest-to-goodness date at a very posh, very public place—the Biltmore. It's a legitimate chance for me to hold you close and not break our agreement."

"But why the Biltmore?" she asked, suddenly remembering her Tuesday meeting there with Derek.

"I need to know—we need to know—what we look like to each other in a different setting from what we've had."

"And it has to be an expensive place like the Biltmore?"

"It sure as hell can't be another boulder."

"And you won't let me say anything about your nonexistent bank balance...."

"Not a word."

How she loved the stubborn set of his jaw—even the quick flare of temper that showed how he really felt when he was trying his best to be refined. "I can hardly wait to dance with you, Mr. Austin." She blew him a kiss. "I don't care very much for all this space between us, either."

"Hold that thought until tonight." He opened the door to go, then looked back at her. "One more thing I discovered while I was at the cabin. I can make love to you just by thinking about it." His laughing, sparkling eyes dared her to question him.

"So we don't need to make love again. We can shut our eyes and recreate everything," she mused, pretending to be serious.

His complicated dappled gaze sent her a silent message of desire. Her body responded with a flood of sensual heat.

"We'll see," he said and shut the door behind him.

Leslie stood at her window, opening it wide so that she could revel in the crisp Santa Barbara air and see the Channel Islands lightly dusted with a veil of fog. Even if it had to be the Biltmore, she wanted any excuse to be with Greg again. But how ironic! Here she was, all ready to talk to him about Indian lore and the things of his natural world, and he was about to put on a suit and try to feel comfortable with a cocktail glass in his hand.

She looked down to see Davy bolting from the house and running pell-mell toward the Jeep. He scrambled into the front seat, lunch box in hand. Before Greg drove off, he wrapped Davy in a bear hug and gave him a kiss. Davy's little arms were just visible around Greg's neck. Leslie could almost read Greg's lips. "I love you, kiddo," he said, and in return Davy kissed him back. They were a team that nothing could break up, Leslie thought. No court in the country could take a child away from such a father. She just hoped she wasn't being naive.

SHE HAD LUNCH with her team at a pleasant fish restaurant near the beach. The Bon Homme project was going well, and the original opinion suvey had already produced excellent responses. They all drank a toast to Justin Reiner with their coffee cups and to themselves.

"Let's do it again soon!" Dorothy Stone said with a nudge to her husband Ed's ribs.

"Hear, hear!" he added. "We've had all the fun and now you have to do the drudgery of analysis. Poor kid."

Leslie laughed, then stopped short when her eyes fixed on a side booth across the room. Greg was there in animated conversation with a handsome woman. He looked happy to be with her. Her heart froze, then she forced herself to stop acting like a soap opera heroine. Of course Greg had other acquaintances, other teachers from college, even old female friends. He hadn't decorated the Seaview all by himself.

"Why don't we all have dinner Tuesday night," Jan was saying, "after it's all over. We can celebrate someplace really nice. I hate just going our own separate ways after this."

Leslie snapped out of her reveries. "It's a good idea, but I have an appointment I can't break. We'll keep in touch—don't worry." She wished earnestly that she could be with them tomorrow night and not with Derek. "Thanks a lot, anyway. I'll be thinking of you. And we still have one more day together for the survey. I'll be in town until Friday finishing my evaluation for Mr. Reiner's computers. If I need to take a breather, I'll give you all a call and we can do something frivolous. Now let's get back to our posts and spread some of this great enthusiasm around the city."

The Seaview Inn had never looked more beautiful to Leslie's admiring eyes when she pulled her car into the driveway. The afternoon sunlight was at a magical angle that made the old gingerbread building come to life. On top of the tower's conical roof the eagle weather vane gleamed, ready to take flight with a bright brass arrow in its claws. The cream and sky-blue colors of the house sparkled and the decorative wooden spindlework under the many eaves looked like fine lace.

Ofelia opened the front door before Leslie could turn the key. "Señor Austin and Davy will be home soon. They go to the Botanic Gardens for Davy's acorns. I am so happy that he take you out for dinner tonight," she said. "He tell me not to worry—he will treat you right."

"And I'll be nice to him, too," Leslie assured her.

Ofelia leaned close, as if in confidence. "The last time he wear his suit is two years ago when he meet with the city about a license for the inn. This must be very special, no?"

Leslie replied with caution. "Just a date with a friend."

"Okay, just a date." Ofelia grinned and gave her an enveloping hug. "Have a good time."

Upstairs Leslie dressed, taking a long time to wrap her hair into a perfect twist at her nape. She felt like a high school girl going out on her first date. Her one evening dress was sea-green chiffon that tied over one shoulder like a toga and hung in a myriad of tiny soft pleats to her knees. Silver stockings and pale gray sandals finished the outfit. Her tanned arms and graceful shoulders set the look off well, but she wished she had something that matched Greg's style better. *Not exactly Earth Mother.* She frowned.

Just before eight o'clock, the appointed hour, she was standing in the dim light of the parlor, trying not to feel so eager. Picking up one of Greg's California bird books, she marveled at the sheer number of different species. What in the world must a hairy woodpecker look like? A note remarked that it hadn't been seen on the coastal plain since 1928. According to the charts, the acorn woodpecker was here all year round.

She smiled thinking of the Botanic Garden and its creatures, and all the acorns that made a certain woodpecker's existence almost too easy.

"Leslie?" Greg called softly from the doorway. She turned to find him staring at her. "You look... beautiful," he murmured, as if he didn't quite recognize the woman in his parlor.

"Thank you, señor. And may I compliment you on your elegant suit?" If she seemed different in his eyes, he was equally surprising to her. Gone was the California casual look, replaced by a well-tailored gray suit that made him look as though he'd stepped out of a sophisticated fashion magazine. He wouldn't appreciate hearing her say that, she knew.

He took a step toward her and brushed a kiss across her temple. "Did I tell you how much I've thought about you all day? I didn't even have the heart to torment my students with pop quizzes. Now shall we see if the Biltmore has our reservations waiting?"

He led her to the Jeep and gallantly handed her in. The seat had been polished and the toolbox was missing. "I like your car," she teased.

"The old horse didn't know what to think when I washed it this afternoon." He gunned the motor and started the long drive down Anacapa toward the oceanfront. "Hand holding allowed," he said confidently and closed his large, comforting hand around hers. "You really are very beautiful," he said again, lifting her hand to his lips for a kiss. "Among your many other virtues."

Fifteen minutes later they pulled into the parking area of the Biltmore, which sat graciously on a low rise just back from the beach. Its deep archways, red-tiled roofs and rough white stucco walls created the impression of a hacienda welcoming its visitors in the days of the Spanish dons of California.

Inside the spacious, warm-hued lobby the atmosphere was festive. Well-dressed couples strolled in from their cottages on the hotel grounds and somewhere a mariachi band was playing traditional Mexican music.

Greg and Leslie walked past the lounge and dark, crowded bar then along a heavily beamed corridor to the Fountain Court where dinner was being served in elegant style beneath the evening stars. They were shown to a table for two next to a lovely three-tiered stone fountain with water trickling lazily from tier to tier.

"I have to admit I like it," Leslie said softly, noticing the antique lanterns on the square white pillars and the dark heavy beams overhead. Around the base of the fountain were pots of yellow chrysanthemums, adding to the feeling that all the diners in the charming tiled court were really personal guests of the unseen don who owned this place.

Greg took her hand again and held it while they studied their menus. "I have a jaundiced eye. I had my fill of black tie dinners and champagne receptions when I was married. It made me intolerant of pretense—the wine-and-brie mentality."

"Let me guess. You never learned to be a wine snob, right?"

"My father-in-law tried to teach me, but he soon found out I was hopeless. He always thought I was a poor hick that Celeste dragged in from the wilds. He still does. Let's order before I think too much about Paul Hartshorn."

"I don't know why I like you so much," Leslie said and entwined her fingers around his, smiling as she did.

"Damned if I know, either."

The waiter took their order and asked if they wanted wine. Greg looked ruefully at Leslie. "Why don't you choose something?"

Leslie glanced down the list, noticing the selection was a good one. Derek made it a point to know the intimate stories of all the French and Californian vineyards, year by year, and a little of his knowledge had rubbed off on her. What went well with sea bass and sole amandine? "We'll have the Muscadet '83." She knew it would be good with fish and wasn't too expensive.

"What is it?" Greg asked after the waiter had gone.

"Just a modest little white wine from France. You don't have to be a snob to like it, I promise."

"How's your survey coming? I've been rude not to ask before."

"As well as could be expected, under the circumstances."

"I feel guilty for keeping you up nights." He looked deep into her eyes. "No, I don't. Are you really leaving Friday?"

"Unless you want to hire me at a good salary. I do have to eat."

He brought her hand to his lips while he spoke. "I'll feed you. For as long as you want to stay. You can earn your keep by collecting acorns with me at night."

"That sounds wonderful," Leslie said, "and very unwise."

Greg threw back his head and laughed. "Tell me when we've behaved wisely. You can't."

"That's not true," she objected quickly. "What we're doing now is wise. We've pulled back, we've tried to give ourselves room to breathe."

Greg's face became serious all at once. "Live with me, Leslie. Don't go back to Los Angeles. Let's work at this thing together and see if it leads to something more. Is that a bad suggestion?"

She didn't know the answer to that question, but what he proposed wasn't the way to solve their problem. "I've never lived with a man, Greg—not with Derek, not with anyone. I may look like a modern girl with trendy values, but down deep I'm as conservative as my grandmother." She lowered her voice for emphasis. "And so are you, my dear lover, in case you didn't know it. It's a bad idea all around, but thanks for the invitation. Part of me would have enjoyed it a lot."

He sighed and let go of her hand as the waiter presented the endive-and-hearts-of-palm salads.

"We'll find ways to be together," Leslie said. "Lots of people have commuter romances these days."

"Weekends," he grunted. "Great. And what kind of bed-and-breakfast host would I be then? Weekends are usually my busiest times, but I'd want to be locked up in the tower with you wrapped around me." He looked pained, waiting for her to say something.

"What does Davy think about such goings-on?"

"I've never brought a woman into the house."

She picked at a curly leaf of endive. "I don't think he would understand. Even if I came on weekends, what would he be thinking? A new mommy? And what if I stopped coming? He doesn't deserve to lose again."

"Hell," he muttered. "We're too decent for our own good. Of course I wouldn't do that to him. Maybe I'm subconsciously preparing to lose him and still have something to hold on to."

"You mean, if you return from Philadelphia without Davy, you'll still have me," she said gently, realizing that Greg was exposing his innermost fears freely to her.

"Well, would I have you? What do you think?" His eyes were clouded with pain.

"I've never felt this way about a man before. I don't know if this is what love is, or if I'm caught up in an obsession. I know I don't dare take a leap of faith and quit my good job."

"That's an honest answer. Not the one I wanted to hear, but I'm not in a position to offer you anything better. Let's drop the whole thing for now and just enjoy being together tonight."

Leslie forced herself to smile. "We're awfully good at being tragic lovers. After all, I don't live on the other side of the world. And we have time, lots of time."

The fish course came, and the white wine. They ate but said very little, their eyes making eloquent, silent commentary to their shared thoughts. Finally, with half their dinner still uneaten, Greg put down his fork and said, "I want to hold you . . . right now. Let's have dessert and coffee in the bar and dance."

Greg signaled the waiter and arranged to have the check transferred to the bar. They walked the short distance across the courtyard, where a dance combo was playing music of the forties and couples were swaying slowly on the small dance floor.

Leslie slipped easily into Greg's arms, trying not to shiver with the joy of having his body against hers again. "Hmm," they both said together, then laughed, as they stood in the middle of the floor, not moving for a while, simply savoring the feeling.

"I like the way you dance," Leslie murmured against his shoulder.

"Just don't move your thighs any more than you are, or we'll have to leave this polite company," he warned and cradled her hand against his heart. They danced, more or less, for a long time, sitting down for coffee and sherry trifle dessert only when the band took its break. "I can see why some people are advocating celibacy lately. It certainly tunes the senses to a high pitch," he said with a laugh.

She shook her head and frowned playfully. "I doubt that's the only reason people are celibate. Anyway, you haven't even gone two days in that exalted state."

"Don't be so smart, my darling Les. Before you came along I hadn't been with a woman for six months. I was burned out on quick encounters in ladies' apartments and I didn't like the kind of man I'd become. I was leaving my roots and racking up a lot of guilt along the way."

"You never needed to prove anything."

"It took a while to realize that. Then I holed up and tried to get myself back in order. That was before you walked into my life."

They danced till midnight, when common sense told them that they had to get some sleep one of these nights, as boring as that sounded. Back home, holding their shoes, they tiptoed past Ofelia's room and up the stairs, where they lingered over a good-night kiss.

"I've never tried sleeping standing up," he whispered against her lips. "What about it?"

"Wouldn't work." She smiled and bit down softly on his upper lip. "One of us would collapse and there we'd be, back in a horizontal position."

"Horizontal is bad for us," he groaned, stroking his hand along her back and buttocks and pulling her tight against him.

"Good night," she said and drew back. "Let's give us one more day of clear-headedness before we dive back into insanity. I need to see Derek Parsons and settle things between us one final time."

"I admit that bothers me."

"Give me credit, *señor*."

Greg held her face with his large hands. "Don't forget me when you're with him. Remember everything that's so special about us—how we are together."

"Trust, Greg. Trust," she said, looking straight into his questioning gaze.

"Just so I'll have something to grind my teeth about tomorrow night, where are you meeting him?"

She smiled. "The Biltmore. And don't glare at me like that. Everything's going to be fine. I'll just talk to him for a few minutes and that's it."

"Judas priest, Les. A hotel?"

"Trust me, Greg."

His glare transformed itself into a wicked grin. He took the key from her hand and thrust it decisively into the lock. Scooping her off her feet, he kicked the door shut behind them.

"What are you doing? You're crazy." But she laughed with him.

"I'm going to make sure you don't forget me, my lady."

"Wait, Greg . . ." she said ineffectually as he lightly kissed the place just below her earlobe, then touched a dozen more kisses on her eyelids, her nose, her forehead. Still holding her in his arms, he marched over to the high canopied bed and placed her in the middle of it.

"Greg," she warned, when he pinioned her hands to her sides and leaned his face close to hers.

Slowly his lips came to hers in the lightest of touches, loving and promising. Involuntarily she shivered at the delightful contact and she felt him smile against her lips.

"That was what I wanted to feel. Now I know you won't forget."

She started to laugh again.

"What's so funny?"

"You, for being so melodramatic. And for thinking I'd want to stay a minute longer than I had to at the Biltmore tomorrow."

He released her hands, kissing each palm as he did. "I thought you were going to praise me for my control."

"Good night, *señor*," she said and tossed a pillow after his retreating back. She thought again. "No. Come back. There's one more thing...."

He warily approached the bed, expecting another pillow, but instead Leslie held her arms out to him.

"I'm not a man of steel," he cautioned. "I'd better leave."

"I don't want Superman, I just want you, Greg."

He stood hesitating, not wanting to make a mistake at this point in their game plan.

She twined her fingers with his and drew him down to the welcoming depths of her soft bed. Feeling his racing heart against her breasts, she knew it was all right.

10

"YOU HAVE A NICE TIME last night?" Ofelia asked as she poured Leslie's juice.

She nodded and took a sip. "Dinner was good, but not as good as your home cooking."

"Everyone happy?" Her brown eyes followed Leslie's every move.

"I think so," Leslie replied.

"Señor Austin has early meeting with Señor Vargas today. He leave this for you." She set a folded piece of graph paper in front of Leslie's plate and watched as Leslie read it.

I do trust you, Leslie. Call me if you need me.

"Thanks." Leslie smiled politely and put the note into her skirt pocket. Buttering a piece of corn bread, she asked casually, "Isn't Davy coming down for breakfast?"

"Davy go with his father. I think they want to practice what is going to happen in Philadelphia." On the last word, her voice broke and tears rolled down her broad face.

Leslie stood and embraced her. "I don't believe any judge in the world would separate Mr. Austin and Davy."

"Pray to God." Ofelia pulled away and crossed herself. Then she abruptly bustled over to the stove and busied herself, keeping her back to Leslie. "How you like your eggs today—scrambled or fried?"

"Scrambled, thanks," Leslie murmured distractedly. Philadelphia wasn't any different from Santa Barbara or Los Angeles, she was assuring herself. There were compassionate people everywhere.... There just had to be.

THE FINAL DAY of the survey project flew. By three o'clock the goodbyes and embraces were over, and the survey team's notebooks and materials were stored safely in the trunk of Leslie's car. She drove slowly back to the Seaview, composing in her mind the eloquent but simple speech she would deliver tonight. If Derek insisted on pretending they still had a relationship after that, she would not allow any more emotional blackmail.

Davy was sitting on the bottom step of the front porch when Leslie drove up. He waved and ran toward her. "We've gotta go get my acorns," he said urgently.

"I thought you and your father got them yesterday."

"Yesterday we just got 'em out of the creek and left 'em to dry on top of the big rock. Tomorrow's my show-and-tell." He sounded close to tears.

Leslie sighed and reached over to open the passenger door of her car. "Hop in. I just hope those acorn woodpeckers haven't gotten there before us," she commented with a tender smile.

"Hope not. Dad says they're real hungry birds."

Waiting in the car while Davy ran to collect his acorns, she breathed deeply of the complicated scents of the hills and vowed that she would know the names of every fragrant herb and bush by this time next year. Davy returned looking like a woodland elf—red hair, yellow tennis shoes, the gunnysack he carried encrusted with oak leaves and dirt.

"We'll have to tuck that in a corner of my trunk, Davy." Leslie nodded toward his small burden.

All the way home, Davy talked nonstop about his acorn project. Leslie was slightly relieved to see two boys waiting for Davy at the inn; all his excitement was wearing her out. The three boys ran off chasing a soccer ball. "See ya later!" Davy yelled back, "And thanks!"

Leslie retrieved her heavy load of documents and notebooks from the trunk and went inside, telling herself she must make a second trip to get Davy's gunnysack. But reaching her room, Leslie was met by a note asking her to call the L.A. office.

Justin's secretary, Marie, answered Leslie's call. According to her, Justin was gone for the day, and he'd wanted to speak with Leslie. "You must be having a great time up in Santa Barbara," she remarked wistfully. "We all envy you."

"It's beautiful, Marie, just lovely. Tell Justin I'll call him first thing in the morning, will you?"

"Sure. Bring me back a bottle of clean air," she joked.

Returning to her room, Leslie immersed herself for the next two hours in survey analysis. She knew she wouldn't be doing any constructive work later tonight, after the Biltmore. Besides, she found putting her mind to meeting the demands of a tough assignment— sorting out subjectivity from objectivity—stimulating. When she completed any task, she wanted to know that it was well done.

At six o'clock she heard Greg's old Jeep sputter and stall, then coast to a stop at the side of the house. _All's right with the world_, she thought, smiling. She straightened her pile of papers and used her tape recorder as a paperweight. She couldn't work anymore; her speech to Derek was interfering with her concentration. Phrases were speaking themselves in her mind, overlapping words from the interview tape. But it would all be over and done with in a few hours, she thought gratefully. By ten o'clock tonight she would be in Greg's arms again.

The sea-green cocktail dress hung expectantly in the armoire, but Leslie ignored it and reached for the light-blue cotton shirtwaist. She wanted to look self-assured, strong, not vulnerable. Derek was a smart enough lawyer that he'd read the message right away. They might even settle things in five minutes, sparing Leslie the ordeal of a long dinner with him. On that positive thought she dressed quickly.

As much as she wanted to appear drab and uninteresting tonight, she couldn't; it was a matter of pride. The turquoise earrings belonged with the dress and the lavender eye shadow, too. But these were her only concessions to glamour.

A glance at her watch told her she would make it on time if she hurried. She picked up her small blue shoulder bag and, with one last look back at the serene beauty of her lovely retreat, left the room.

Downstairs, Leslie almost careened into a middle-aged couple who were entering the inn. "Pardon me," she apologized.

"Are you the proprietor?" the man asked.

"No, but he should be here any minute...." She sidled past them. As the door closed behind her, she heard Greg's booming deep voice greeting his new guests.

GREG WATCHED Leslie disappear out the front door and he felt helpless and frustrated. The Fergusons were waving their confirmation letter in his face, expecting immediate attention. He tried to be charming, but his heart was still reacting to the glimpse of a turquoise earring and the swirl of light blue skirt.

While the couple signed the register, Greg watched the old Mustang pull out of the driveway and head down Anacapa Street. Leslie looked good, he thought miserably, too good.

"If you'll just show us to our room we'll say goodnight," Mr. Ferguson was saying.

"My pleasure," Greg murmured, leading the way upstairs to the room recently vacated by the Silverwoods. He left them raving about the Victorian double bed and came back a few minutes later with the tray of sherry glasses.

"Couldn't be nicer," Mrs. Ferguson complimented. "We're going to have a light supper and then sleep like babies in this room. Could you recommend a good little restaurant nearby?"

"All the information you'll need is in that packet by your bed, ma'am. There's a list of the best places for a reasonable meal and of interesting things to do in Santa Barbara. I'll leave you now. Good night and sleep well."

He could barely contain himself—he wanted to do one last errand. There was still one glass of sherry on his tray.

Leslie's room felt alive with her presence. He stood over her bed imagining her there. He set the little glass on the bedside table, noticing the neat pile of work, the briefcase propped against the table leg. Her handwriting, fine and strong on the pages of numbers and cryptic notations, spoke to him of strength, passion . . . determination. He was a fool to expect her to walk away from her career for him. Her dedication to her work was one aspect of her he had taken much too lightly.

On impulse he picked up the tape recorder, slipped an unused tape into the machine and pressed the play/ record button. "My darling Les," he whispered as the tape started turning, "it's seven-thirty and I miss you already."

LESLIE WALKED SMARTLY to the entrance of the Biltmore bar where the dance combo was tuning up for their first set. The room was dark and buzzing with predinner cocktail activity. She edged her way past several unattached men who gave her appreciative glances. She saw a hand wave at her from the corner booth and recognized the dimly lit face of Derek. She took a deep breath and pressed on.

"Darling!" he called out when she was close enough to hear. He stood and wrapped her in a crushing embrace, kissing her unresponsive mouth before letting her go. "Let's get out of here," he shouted above the din. "I have a quiet table in the lounge." He picked up his martini—vodka, never gin—and led her by the hand out of the bar.

Several steps down from the lobby they entered the lounge, a large room with dark ceiling beams, brass lamps and potted trees discretely arranged to give an intimate feeling to the clusters of upholstered wing chairs and sofas. They walked to the far end of the carpeted room where a love seat faced the impressive fireplace. A fire had been set but was not yet burning.

"This is much better," Derek declared, and motioned for service. "You look awfully beautiful to these love-starved eyes. Don't ever do this to me again, darling . . . promise." He stared intently into her eyes.

Leslie remembered only then that Derek's eyes were brown—just plain brown—with no dancing lights, no depth.

"Tell me you missed me," he prodded when she didn't respond.

"I've thought a lot about you . . . about us," she began.

He reached out a finger to touch her lips. "No, no," he chided. "Wrong words. Just watch my lips. He mouthed I missed you, Derek, exaggerating the motions.

"Derek, I think you know why I came tonight, and it wasn't to play games," she said, pulling back from his touch. He was wearing Ralph Lauren's Polo cologne as usual, but this was the first time she had found it unpleasant. She knew he was wearing it for her; she had given him a bottle of it for his birthday.

A waiter appeared with a tray of hors d'oeuvres, and Derek ordered drinks for both of them, saying, "The lady will have vermouth and cassis on ice with a twist. And tell the maître d' that we'll want our table in ten minutes."

Derek put one arm around Leslie's shoulder and leaned back, taking her with him. "You're awfully quiet, my love. Tired? I told your boss he was working you too hard. That may be fine for some people but not for my Leslie." He breathed close to her ear and kissed it. "I've got better plans for your future."

Leslie reached for a cheese puff. "Don't, Derek. You sound as if things weren't already settled between us. They are." She was ready to start her speech and get it over with.

He smiled and turned her stiff-jawed face toward him. "Let's not have our little talk right now, all right? We always do better after a good meal and a bottle of excellent wine."

"You aren't making it easy for me," she said softly.

"Why should I? I'm a good lawyer. Strategy is my forte. There's a right time for everything, and our right time is about ten o'clock tonight, over some espresso and cognac. *Then* we'll talk." His handsome face wore an expression that denied rebuttal.

"But you know what I'm going to tell you," she argued.

"Yes, I know. But that shouldn't keep us from enjoying our evening, no matter what the outcome. Anyway, I wanted to make sure you remembered what a nice guy I was." He grinned and winked.

Leslie couldn't help smiling at his pressure tactics. "So be it. Just don't be angry if things don't turn out the way you want."

He shrugged his impeccably clad shoulders. "I leave it up to the gods. Now let's toast to Leslie and Derek, together again."

Leslie took her drink from the waiter. "I'd rather toast to the best for each of us, no matter what."

He chuckled knowingly. "I forgot how defensive you can be, but it just makes me love you all the more."

Leslie sipped her drink, regretting that she hadn't been quick enough to divert Derek's determined path for the evening. What wishful thinking to imagine she could finish their business in a few minutes. Derek was a very smart man—a fighter.

She looked up at the heavily framed portrait hanging above the fireplace. A young Spanish prince stared down at her, expressionless and pale in his burgundy velvet and satin costume. Suddenly she felt trapped by the opulence and expectations of a world she wanted to move away from. Derek was talking on and on about his law practice and how pleased the senior partners were with his work, but Leslie heard only the tone of his voice—ambitious, self-satisfied, aggressive....

"And how is your job coming along?" he asked finally, then emptied his drink. "Are all your little people behaving themselves?"

Leslie bristled. "The members of my team are delightful. They've worked hard and done beautifully."

"One thing I prize in you is your organizational ability. I see it in your talent for pulling together a dinner party on short notice. You're a jewel among women, my love. Now let's go and test the mettle of the Biltmore's executive chef, shall we?"

Dinner progressed uneasily, with Derek's attention taken up with the wine list and a running commentary on the quality of the food. Leslie knew she would have to cut this charade short and be firm, direct and final. She had already let Derek go too far.

She stole glances at him as they ate, wondering how she could have thought his too-perfect face truly handsome. And his smooth manicured hands—they were weak, not the kind that would pick up a log or fix a leaky pipe... or caress her body until it sang with pleasure.

"Remember that night at Scandia," he was saying, "after we saw that marvelously offbeat play at the Ahmanson? You were quiet then, too. But everything worked out later, didn't it?"

He was no fool. Of course she remembered having let him talk her into going to Seattle to meet her family.

He knew he would make a good impression, that her mother would love him. He was polite, intelligent, had a good future, and he had showered her with compliments and gifts.

She pushed her dinner plate away. "It's time, Derek. We have to talk, and all this reminiscing is a waste of energy."

"I agree," he said. "But we can't talk here. We'll be far more comfortable in my cottage. I've arranged for our espresso to be brought there."

"Madame?" Derek offered his arm and Leslie reluctantly took it. She could have insisted that they talk in the lobby, but in the mood he was in tonight, Derek was capable of making a scene. She hated emotional scenes in public.

They walked under a Spanish-style archway that led back to the gardens and the private cottages, which were spaced around the grounds—peaceful refuges from the busy world. Derek opened the door to one of the small buildings and stood aside for her to enter.

Fresh bouquets of flowers covered the low coffee table and the standing bar. Through an arched doorway Leslie saw an arrangement of red roses on the bedside table. "Make yourself comfortable, Leslie," he said. "And while you're at it, you might open the envelope on the coffee table. Coffee should be on its way."

"If it's the plane ticket, I'd rather not open it. Why didn't you cancel the reservation?" She was becoming annoyed.

"Open," he said mysteriously.

She perched on the edge of a sofa cushion and lifted the flap of the large white envelope that bore the travel agency logo, while Derek answered the knock at the door. She didn't need to examine the ticket. But she stiffened when she saw the small jeweler's box.

A waiter brought in a tray and set it down on the coffee table, then left, well tipped. "Don't open the box yet, darling," he ordered gently. "Just leave it there while we talk."

What should have taken five minutes took three hours. Derek refused to accept Leslie's decision, not even after she looked him straight in the eye and said, "No, Derek. I'm not going to marry you. I'm not in love with you." In response, he wove intellectual webs around each of her reasons until tears of frustration threatened.

"You haven't heard anything I've said," she breathed.

"Every word. But you don't mean them—that's what I've been trying to show you," he said soothingly. "Darling Leslie, don't you understand—we're the perfect team. We have to be married, and soon. Everything else depends on it."

Her mind cleared abruptly. "What do you mean, everything else?"

"The partnership, of course." He looked slightly surprised at her lack of understanding.

"Ah, the partnership," she repeated. "What partnership, Derek?" She wanted to force him to be honest, for once.

He looked warily at her cool expression. "I shouldn't have mentioned it. The important thing is that I love you. And as soon as we're married—"

"Is that why you've been pushing me so hard . . . I'm part of some grand plan for you to become a partner in your law firm?" Her voice was icy and she stood to leave.

"No, not exactly," he faltered. "It was just a matter of timing. We were going to be married, anyway, so why not December?"

"Didn't I deserve to know your plans?" The whole headlong courtship was making sense to her for the first time.

"Dammit, Leslie, we have to be married before the committee considers my promotion in December."

"And they don't give partnerships to unmarried men, is that it? Is that the secret behind this mad dash into matrimony?" She saw his face lose its expression of bravado. She reached for her purse.

"Come on, Leslie, don't be foolish. It's a damnably conservative firm. They want stable family men. I told them we—"

"Tell them the lady refused the generous offer," she shot back. "Damn you, Derek Parsons, how dare you use me or any woman! The word is no—N-O," she spelled out. "Is that clear enough?" She pushed past him and threw open the door, then looked back and added, "I'll bet you don't even know what a hairy woodpecker is!"

She strode away from him along the winding garden path knowing that he was standing in the doorway watching her. Did a twinge of loss ruffle his well-protected heart, or was he merely angry because she had let him down—spoiled all his careful plans? Without a backward glance, she rounded a bend in the walkway and was free of him forever, except for the churning irritation in her stomach.

11

GREG WAS SITTING in his battered leather chair nursing a cold cup of coffee when the hall clock struck eight-thirty. For the past hour he'd gone over and over the numbers on his slippage analysis for the Piggott's Mesa job, and they still didn't add up right. His mind was otherwise occupied, picturing Leslie at the Biltmore, wondering how long it took to tell someone adios.

The phone rang, snapping him to attention and making his heart lurch. A cordial voice said, "Would you connect me with Leslie O'Neill's room, please. It's Justin Reiner here."

"I'm sorry, she's out," Greg said. "I can take a message and make sure she sees it when she gets in."

"Tell her I'm returning her call. We haven't been able to connect. Her family's been trying to contact her and couldn't, so they asked me to. I don't know how important this is."

"I'll let her know."

"Thanks. Are you the proprietor of the inn?"

"Yes."

"Leslie told me how much she's enjoying your establishment. Thanks again. Good night."

Greg hung up, thinking Justin Reiner sounded like a good guy. Leslie was lucky to have him as a boss.

He looked over at the corner of his desk where Leslie's little tape machine sat, reminding himself to return it to her room before she got home. He had half a mind to erase everything he'd put onto the tape; it made him uncomfortable to bare his feelings like that. Hell, he thought, it made him uncomfortable just sitting here caring so much for Leslie.

He reached for the phone again and dialed a number in Ventura. "Arnold Murchison, please," he said and waited. He had to get out of the house for a while, and old man Murchison always loved to talk about his development plans for the Mesa.

"Mr. Murchison? Greg Austin. How about a confab tonight? I've got some interesting map work to show you. Another fifteen minutes and it'll be finished. You said you wanted it as soon as possible."

Listening to the voice on the other end, Greg could always smell the bad cigars that the canny old man always smoked. "I was just thinkin' about you, son," he said. "Sure, come on down. The wife's goin' to bed, but I'm a night owl. I was just about to break out a bottle of my best brandy."

On his way down to Ventura, Greg had resisted taking the small detour from the highway that would have led to the parking lot of the Biltmore Hotel. He had too much pride to go snooping around looking for her. Anyway, what if he ran into Leslie with that guy? He'd look like a perfect ass.

Now it was almost midnight and he was heading back to the inn again—home to Leslie, he hoped. Arnold Murchison had been pleased with his work on the

Mesa project and had paid him a fat bonus for finding the underground water source. It was turning out to be a pretty fair night, after all.

But he couldn't leave well enough alone. Too much of old man Murchison's homemade brandy had made its way down Greg's throat tonight, taking the good sense out of him. He knew the moment he turned the Jeep off the highway toward the Biltmore Hotel parking lot that it was a stupid thing to do.

Greg found the white Mustang parked, and empty, and his eyes blurred for a split second. He felt as if a mule had kicked him in the gut and left the hoof behind. He pulled in next to her car and sat there, his mind clouded with images of Leslie. Where the hell was she? He'd been drinking but he wasn't drunk and he caught himself just short of leaving the car and crashing around the hotel grounds searching for her. *She can come home when she damned well wants to*, he thought, as he gathered up his pride and started the Jeep.

LESLIE WALKED SWIFTLY AWAY from the hotel gardens and toward the beach. She was upset with Derek and with her own explosive reaction to him. And she wasn't in any shape to return home and see Greg again. Not yet.

Phosphorous light danced along the crests of the low, lapping waves and the misty waning moon hung close to the horizon. She walked slowly to the very end of the long Biltmore pier and leaned over the railing, waiting for her nerves to calm. Behind her, in the distance, was the hotel with its lights and activity, but here it was peaceful.

So Derek had been shopping for a wife. She might have been any female with a pleasing appearance and social skills. How she could have been so blind, she wondered, so taken in by the insincerity. That would never happen again, she swore.

After a while she left the pier and stepped onto the sandy beach with her shoes and stockings in hand. A long way south of the hotel she sat down at the edge of the water with her knees pulled up under her chin, feeling no sense of victory with the outcome of the evening. She wished Derek happiness, however he defined it.

All she wanted now was the down-to-earth sanity of her love for Greg Austin. Tired as she was, she longed for the safe haven of his arms. *He'll laugh when I tell him how it all came out,* she thought as she walked back toward the hotel grounds and her waiting car.

The drive to the Seaview Inn was like coming home after a long exile. Her heart was beating fast as she turned her key in the front door lock and entered the silent hall.

She had expected to see a light under Greg's office door, but it was dark. The whole house was dark. Then she smiled. Of course—he was in the tower waiting for her. She quietly mounted the curving stairway to the third floor and knocked at his door. "The prodigal has returned," she whispered close to the door.

A long moment later it opened and Greg stood before her, fully dressed and unsmiling. A thick wall of energy prevented her from reaching out to touch him.

"Is something wrong?" she asked, paralyzed before the odd force field that separated them.

"I can't take it, Les. I'm better off alone." His face looked gray even in the near-darkness of the doorway.

"What are you talking about?" she demanded, caught completely off balance by his response to her.

"I'm jealous as hell and I'm not going to get any better. That's what I'm talking about."

"Greg . . ." She extended one hand toward him. "It's all over. Derek is out of my life forever."

"There'll be others. Someday there'll be others. And I can't take it." He turned away from her and went to one of the tall windows.

Leslie was dumbstruck. "What about the trust you promised? Don't you think you're being insulting?" She wasn't going to let him get away with his idiotic statements.

"I don't know if I want to be so . . . so . . . connected to you. I care so damned much it takes all the life out of me," he said in a ragged whisper. "For God's sake— it's one in the morning! What did you think I was doing all this time—making lesson plans for my students? I've been turning myself inside out."

Leslie went slowly to him and touched his shoulder. "I need you tonight, of all nights, Greg. Won't you hold me . . . please? Just put your arms around me and hold me. Everything's going to be fine now. You've got to believe it."

He didn't turn around. "It won't work, Les," he murmured.

She stared at his stubborn back and refused to give up. "That's not how I expected to be greeted. I thought we had something stronger than that. Dumb as it sounds now, I was even thinking of commitment," she said softly.

"Commitment," he grunted. "I'm a bad bet."

"Greg Austin, turn around this instant!" she ordered. "You're wallowing in some drama out of your past and you should be ashamed! My name is Leslie, not Celeste. If you so much as *think* I'm like her I'll...I'll throw you through this window!"

He leaned against the window frame and said nothing for a moment. Then he started to laugh—a loud laugh from the depths of his chest. For the first time his eyes met hers fully. "Oh, Miss O'Neill, you're one tough lady. You know how to cut me right down to size." He wrapped her in his powerful arms and held her against him. How good it felt. "I don't want to let you out of my sight ever again, Les." He nuzzled her hair. "Why don't you marry me and put me out of my misery?"

She drew in her breath and let it out slowly. "Don't kid about something as serious as that, Greg."

"I'm not kidding. Think about it—it's perfect," he said, his voice becoming more and more animated. "I've been scared as a rabbit about marriage again, but maybe I was being blind to the best thing I ever had. That's you, Les. Let's do it." His eyes were fixed on hers.

Leslie gently pushed him away; she had to have room to think. "Tell me again," she started cautiously. "You were jealous because I was out late with Derek, so upset that you weren't capable of even thinking about commitment. Then all of a sudden something changed your mind, and you want to get married. What was that, Greg? I have to know. And please, if you care at all, be absolutely honest with me."

Greg sobered quickly. "Am I supposed to have hidden motives? Like what?"

"Like finding a wife and mother for your little family just in time for Philadelphia. Or am I being cynical? Yours is the second marriage proposal I've had tonight that made me feel like a useful item to ensure a man's future plans, and that's not very heartwarming."

"Don't say that," he warned. "I wasn't thinking anything at all, except that I really need you. All the rest was the brandy talking. I was down in Ventura for a while, giving Murchison my Mesa report. I'm not much of a drinker." He looked apologetic.

She wouldn't be put off. "Need isn't love."

Greg's gaze wavered. "I have a twitch about that word, Les."

"It isn't easy for me, either," she said quietly. "But I always thought that when the right time came, it would be as natural to say as any other word. This can't be the right time for either of us."

His green eyes clouded. "What do you want, then?"

She sighed wearily, sadly. "Something absolutely real and rock solid. There were times these past days when I thought we had just that—or at least we were on our way to having it."

"You're saying no?"

"Ask me again when you can say the right words and mean them." Her face was tight from the effort not to weep in front of him. Her heart felt like a live coal inside her chest.

Greg ran his hand through his hair distractedly and turned away. "I'll be selling the house if I don't get custody of Davy. No use having a home if there's no family to live in it." His voice was flat. "I wouldn't be much of a host to visitors."

"And I'm going to accept the promotion that Justin offered me a few days ago. I don't know where I'll be, but maybe we can keep in touch."

She felt the winding down of their affair, as if it was a giant carousel that was grinding to a halt and had to stop. Her ride with Greg was ending, and she was powerless to change the course of events. Her hands were clenched into fists at her sides. She couldn't remember a more wretched moment in her life. "Olson and Loeb think I've done a good job in Santa Barbara," she stated lamely.

"Congratulations," Greg offered lamely. "Send me a card." He was silent for a moment before he turned back to her. "Will you do me one favor? When you're off being successful in some other city, don't forget everything about Santa Barbara, okay?"

She couldn't reply. It was all she could do to walk numbly from the tower room and down the curving steps, probably for the last time. Greg didn't stop her.

SHE WAS DRIVING eighty miles an hour on the freeway toward Los Angeles, desperate to put some distance between herself and Santa Barbara. She was hurt, puzzled and just plain tired.

At 3:00 a.m. she entered her basement garage, too spent to bother with her luggage and work materials. She left them locked in the car and walked up the fake terrazzo staircase to her apartment. She dropped onto the pink satin comforter that Derek had given her and willed herself to sleep. Her last conscious thought was of how to explain to Justin that she was doing her final analysis at home, rather than in Santa Barbara. She didn't dare let herself think about Greg.

The telephone rang several times, but she didn't answer it. When it rang again she looked at her watch and snapped awake; it was nearly noon. Justin was no doubt trying to reach her. But it wasn't her boss.

"Leslie, it's Greg. I'm almost out of my mind," he blurted in an urgent voice, not bothering to say hello.

"Look, Greg..."

"Davy's gone, run away. The police won't do anything yet."

"No!" she gasped.

"I've been driving all over hell and back and can't find him anywhere. The school called this morning because he didn't show up in the classroom. He just wandered away from the playground before the first bell. The bus driver said he got off with the other children, but nobody spoke to him after that—" His voice broke and he stopped.

"Maybe he's just hiding somewhere. Did anything happen to upset him this morning?"

"I shouldn't have told him you left without saying goodbye to him. He didn't take it very well, but I wasn't thinking. I shouldn't have said anything. He's not the kind of kid who runs away, though."

"What about his grandparents . . . the custody problem?"

"They could have had somebody take him...or...it could be worse."

"I'm coming up right now," she said without a second thought.

"No, don't. There's no reason for you to . . . I just wanted to tell you. . . . I needed to hear your voice again."

"Greg," she prompted into the heavy silence. "You'll find him, do you understand? And whatever you do, don't be angry with him when he finally comes home."

"Dear God, Les..." he said helplessly, then hung up.

"Let him be safe!" she prayed aloud, replacing the receiver.

Seconds later the phone rang again. "Leslie O'Neill?" a man's voice asked. "This is Anderson down at the Greyhound station. We've got your son here."

"My son?"

"About three feet tall, red hair? Answers to the name of Davy?"

"Yes!"

"You'd better come down and claim him. And bring ticket fare for his joyride. We don't encourage stowaways, ma'am." The voice was not unkind.

She wondered briefly how the man had gotten her phone number, then remembered she'd written it out for Davy the day they'd collected acorns.

Her fingers stumbled over the push buttons as she rushed to call the Seaview Inn. "Greg, I've found him! He's at the L.A. Greyhound station and I'm going there right now."

"Thank God!" he almost shouted. "How fast can you get his little backside up here, Les? All hell's about to break loose."

"I'm leaving as soon as I can get dressed."

"Well, hurry. You can't guess who's coming to the inn this afternoon to evaluate Davy's living conditions . . . an agent of the Philadelphia courts. I've got guests scheduled to arrive any minute, Ofelia's not here today and it's going to be one big mess."

"I'll be there by three at the latest. Calm down. It's going to be all right.

"Of all the luck," she muttered to herself as she threw on a denim skirt and Shetland sweater. Of course the agent would make an unannounced visit; the court wanted to see the real home life of father and son. But why today, of all times?

She raced downtown to the bus station and found Davy in the supervisor's office. She swept him up in her arms and kissed him, then saw to the formalities of paying for his ticket. "We'll talk about everything when we're in the car," she said as she signed the credit card receipt and grabbed his hand to leave.

"You shouldn't've left," Davy said solemnly, once they were out of the parking lot.

"I was about to say the same thing to you, young man. Why did you do such a thing? Your father was worried sick."

He looked at Leslie as if she should know the answer. "You took my acorns. Today was show-and-tell."

"The acorns!" she echoed, horrified. "I forgot to bring your gunnysack into the house yesterday. But that was not a good reason to run away."

"Roger Cranston was gonna make fun of me if I didn't have 'em. I just wanted to get 'em out of your car. Then I was gonna take a bus back home. I guess I didn't know how far it was gonna be."

He looked away quickly and Leslie saw there were tears in his eyes. "Why'd ya go away like that?" he continued on a high, wobbling voice, "I thought you liked me."

Leslie reached out to stroke his head. "Oh, Davy, it wasn't you. I had to get back to my work here much sooner than I expected."

"Well," he said, not quite convinced, "ya should've told me."

Leslie stopped the car and drew the stiff little body to her in a loving embrace. "And that's why you ran away? Not just to get back your acorns?"

He allowed her to hold him, then at last he looked up at her, his face streaked with tears. "You were just gone . . . and Dad didn't say anythin' . . . and . . ."

"I love you, Davy. And I apologize for not telling you I was leaving. It was a terrible thing for a friend to do. Forgive me?" She took a tissue from her purse and wiped his face. "I can't always be in Santa Barbara, but I'll always be your friend. And I'd love to have you write me long letters about what you're doing." She felt awful for hurting him so, selfish and thoughtless.

He rubbed the last of his tears away and smiled. "Why cantcha live in Santa Barbara? It's a lot closer."

"My boss only sent me there for a while on a special job. Now listen, Davy. When we get back to the inn, there are some people visiting this afternoon who want to see how the Austin family lives."

"Are they from Phila...that place?" he asked gravely.

"Yes, but don't be nervous. And don't say a word about today's bus trip. They wouldn't understand."

Leslie drove the familiar route in record time, arriving in front of the old Victorian house just as another car was driving up. A man and woman were inside, jotting notes on their clipboards before leaving their car.

She pulled the Mustang around to the kitchen entrance and rushed inside with Davy, where Greg wrapped him in a huge hug and swatted his bottom. "Don't ever do this to me again, you hear?" he said.

"The Philadelphia people are about to ring the doorbell," Leslie interrupted. "Good luck."

Greg caught the sleeve of her sweater as she turned to go. "You have to stay. Please . . . I don't want to face this alone. It'll look better to have a respectable woman here. Please, Les."

She looked down at her old skirt. "Hardly respectable, but if you need a friend, I'll stay," she agreed.

"Thanks. How about fixing up some tea for our guests?" he asked nervously.

"Answer your door. I'll do what I can. You just get everyone settled in the parlor."

"And you say you're a guest at the Seaview, Miss O'Neill?" the efficient-looking gray haired woman asked after everyone was seated comfortably.

"She's more than a guest," Greg hastened to answer. "A close friend of the family, as well." Davy left his father's side and went to sit cross-legged on the floor next to Leslie.

"I see." The woman nodded. "How nice. And you, Mr. Austin. How much time would you estimate you spend with Davy each day?"

"Enough time for him to know he's got a father who loves him," Greg said abruptly. "I didn't know I was supposed to be keeping a log."

"And you, Davy," she continued, "do you remember your grandparents in Philadelphia?"

Davy looked up at Leslie and then at Greg. "I guess so." He shrugged. "Not very much. I like it better here— a whole lot."

"If I may say something," Leslie volunteered. "There's warmth and love in this house. It was obvious to me the first time I came here, and I hope you can see it, too."

A thin smile moved across the woman's sober lips. The man said nothing, but made quick notations on his pad of paper. "We must look for certain things in the environment that add to or detract from healthy circumstances for the child. Perhaps Davy would like to leave the room for a few minutes while we talk."

Greg motioned to Davy. "Go get yourself some lemonade from the kitchen," he said. "I'll be finished here in a few minutes."

The woman seemed not to notice the defiant tone in his voice. As soon as Davy had left, she proceeded down her list of intrusive and interminable questions.

Leslie felt Greg's mounting irritation. She caught his eye from time to time and tried to be supportive.

Everything he said sounded somehow inadequate. Of course he was a good father, but the pointed questions about his relationship with women—"Are they casual or serious?" "Do women sleep with you in this house?"—brought replies that revealed his simmering belligerence.

Leslie was becoming just as angry at these strangers and their clinical attitude. How would they know what kind of warmth was in this little family? Had they really seen the love that made the old Victorian house into a happy home?

"Has Davy been under the care of a psychologist since his unfortunate removal from his grandparents' house two years ago?"

"Why the hell should he be?" Greg spat. "He's the most normal kid I've ever seen. What do you think? I warped his little mind by taking him away from all the luxury money could buy?"

"Mr. Austin," the woman said patiently. "This isn't a pleasure for us any more than it is for you, but we must ascertain how well you understand the needs of the child."

"Well enough to guarantee that if the court takes him away from this house—away from me—Davy will need more than a psychologist to make him happy again.

That's a promise. If you want to see a warped child, you do just that, lady! You just do that!"

Greg's outburst seemed to make the end of the agonizing interview; the man and woman rose to leave.

"It's been most informative, Mr. Austin. Thank you for your hospitality," the man ventured to say. "Don't show us out, we'll just want to walk around some before we leave."

Greg's tone was explosive. "I'd rather show you out," he said, barely in control of his emotions. "If you have any more questions, you can call my lawyer. I'm sure you have his number in your little black book."

The departure was swift.

Greg stormed back to the parlor. "I blew it, dammit! They pulled it out of me. Paul Hartshorn's money is behind those bloodsuckers—I'd swear to it!"

"Greg, no one can blame you. They were obnoxious," Leslie soothed. "I have to go now. Let me know if I can help." She picked up her purse and keys.

He stood towering over her, looking bleak. His eyes were glistening with emotion. "I don't seem to be able to hang on to anything, do I?"

She pretended not to know what he meant. It would be so very easy to open her arms and invite him in. And he'd come, she knew . . . but for the wrong reasons. "I'll leave Davy's gunnysack and acorns on the back porch. Tell him I'll write him a long letter when I get home."

"Les . . ." he said huskily. "I'm sorry about everything." He smiled his lopsided smile, but his eyes were serious. "I need you tonight. Stay with me."

Her heart ached with her own need to be lost in his strong arms, to laugh again and love again. She couldn't look at him when she answered, "I can't, Greg. Go and give Davy a hug and then call your lawyer." It was difficult trying to sound controlled.

"So that's it, then?"

"I think it has to be . . . for now." If she didn't leave right this minute she would lose her senses and run back to all the sweet pain of loving him.

"So long, Les," he murmured.

"So long," she whispered and, eyes averted, turned toward the door to go.

GREG WAS IMPATIENT with the two rings it took before Jim Vargas answered his phone.

"I've got bad news about my little tea party," he said abruptly when Jim came on to the line. "I just threw my two guests out the door."

"I've got some news, too. Better sit down for this one. You're not going to like it one bit. *¿Compadre?* Are you still there?"

"Yeah, shoot."

"I got a call from the judge's secretary just now. He wants to clear his calendar early so he can go to a legal convention. He's got our case scheduled for Monday."

"But that's only five days away!" Greg exploded. "What's he trying to do?"

"Judges do this all the time," Jim said evenly. "The way I look at it, we won't be any readier for the hearing in ten days than we are right now. Maybe it'll even take some of the stress off you to get it over with."

Greg thought about it for a moment. "Okay, so we do it Monday."

"I'll call them back and confirm. Now tell me what went on at your tea party."

"It was the inquisition all over again, Jim, I swear. How many hours a day do you spend with your son? Do you sleep with a lot of women . . . ? They even had the nerve to ask if I knew how much damage I might have done to Davy by taking him away from the Hartshorns' house two years ago. That's when I blew up."

"They were just testing, and you rose to the bait. Was your lady there to soften the impact?"

"What do you mean, my lady?" Greg growled.

"Oh, come on, old friend, you know who I mean. Ofelia keeps me posted."

"You're a damned busybody, Vargas. But, yes, Leslie was there. And, yes, she made things go better. At least she kept me from throttling those two."

"What are you doing tonight? We need to have one last session together with Davy, though I think he'll be fine. It's you I'm worried about."

LESLIE DROVE HOME with a knot in her stomach. Time was all they needed—lots of blessed time to approach each other the way normal people did. This whole crazy thing was going to take the most serious thinking she had ever done in her life.

The phone was ringing as she opened the door to her apartment. She had a feeling she shouldn't answer it, but she told herself not to be a coward.

"Honey, is that you?" her mother's high, anxious voice demanded.

"Oh, Mother...I wasn't expecting you. Hi." Leslie dropped onto the sofa and tried to reorient her thoughts in a hurry.

"You've been so hard to find these past days. I've been worried sick. What's going on? Is everything all right?"

"I'm fine," Leslie said, trying to sound bright and happy. Her mother always sensed when there was a change in the status quo. "I've been on a job in Santa Barbara and now I'm taking a day off, that's all. How is everything in Seattle?"

"We were sitting here imagining that someone had spirited you away to Timbuktu." She laughed, but there was a hint of accusation behind her words. "Dad and I feel so left out of your life lately, dear."

"I should have called you before I went to Santa Barbara, but everything was happening so fast I didn't get a chance. You know I think about you both," she soothed, hoping to keep away from talk of Derek and the dangers of a single woman living alone.

"And then when Mr. Reiner couldn't find you...you can see why we were concerned. Anyway, we have wonderful news. Dad gave me the most marvelous gift for our thirtieth anniversary. We're going on a cruise! Italy, Greece, Turkey, the Islands, and then a dream trip up the Nile. I'm still in shock!"

Leslie smiled. "Tell Dad he's a dear. That's really great. When do you leave?"

"Tomorrow, if you can imagine such a thing. I don't even have time to get together a proper wardrobe, but

Dad says he'll buy me anything I need when we get to London. He's giving me three days there before we board the ship. Don't you wish you were coming with us?"

"You don't need me," she said. "You deserve your second honeymoon."

There was a pause, then, "Leslie, honey. . . was there anything you wanted to tell me?"

"Not a thing, just bon voyage. I love you both."

"Bye bye, then, dearest," her mother said with an emotional quaver in her voice.

Leslie was happy for her parents' pleasure, but a feeling of relief came with the click on the other end of the line. She changed into her comfortable robe and gave Justin a call at his home. It was well after seven o'clock.

"Just thought you deserved to know where your rookie supervisor was," she said.

"I suppose this has to do with the vagaries of the human heart," he chided gently.

"I've got a pretty good report to make about the survey," she countered. "Give me a day to finish writing it up and then you can scold me all you want."

She heard his indulgent chuckle and the strains of some classical music behind it. "Come see me in the office Friday morning. We can have lunch afterward. Remember I told you there was a plum waiting for you?"

After he'd hung up, Leslie made herself a pot of peppermint tea and curled up in the corner of her sofa for a long evening of mental activity. She had to keep busy or else the mesmerizing images that were pressing against her mind would break loose again: Greg's intent green eyes watching her face at the moment their bodies first came together in love...the delicious sounds they made in the silence of the canyon...the sharp clean smell of mountain sage...Greg looking down at her while the soft dawn light filtered through the trees around their boulder nest....

Her heart constricted painfully. She took a deep breath and reached for a pile of paperwork.

She fell asleep sometime in the middle of the night, her notebooks and typewriter perched precariously on the edge of the sofa. When she awoke again, her jaw ached from tension and she wondered if the pain in her stomach meant that she was flirting with an ulcer. Her refrigerator was almost empty, but it didn't matter as she had no appetite.

During the morning, as she spread out the survey on her little dining room table that substituted for a desk, she noticed that the cassette recorder was missing. Luckily, there wasn't anything important on the tape. *But, still,* her scheming thoughts urged, *it might be a good idea to call Santa Barbara and make sure the recorder is safe.* She stopped herself from reaching out for the telephone. *Not yet...not yet.*

She reached instead for her notebooks and thrust her thoughts back to business. She couldn't allow him to have such control of her. She had to stay away from him long enough to start thinking in a rational manner.

After a long day of concentrated work, she'd finished the report for Justin. Leslie glanced at the kitchen clock. Ten. Ofelia had already put her little chocolate mints on the lace pillowcases. Maybe somebody was taking a long soothing rosemary bath in the room that faced the ocean. Life was going on there without Leslie O'Neill. Her heart yearned for the comfort of that beckoning place as if it were home.

GREG FINISHED GRADING the last of the geology tests and sat back in his dilapidated desk chair. Davy was asleep for the night, Ofelia was still puttering in the kitchen and the couple upstairs in Leslie's old room were tucked in with their sherry. He looked around impatiently at the clutter of his office, trying to convince himself everything was going to be just fine. Jim Vargas seemed confident that the court would rule in Greg's favor... so why did he feel as if he was about to come apart at the seams?

Leslie—it was Leslie. He wanted her here, right now, tangled up with him, wild and warm. He missed her. She belonged here.

Sliding open the center drawer of the desk, he gazed at the little tape recorder. He hadn't treated her the way he should have. If he hadn't been acting like the hind end of a horse... "What a pathetic jerk you are," he growled to himself, rubbing the stubble of his beard. "You deserve to lose her."

He picked up the tape machine and pressed the Record button. Keeping his voice to a rough whisper he began to talk.

12

LESLIE WAS UP EARLY and reading her report for Olson and Loeb one more time, wondering what she should do about her state of mind. Did she really want to sever the bittersweet cord that connected her to Greg Austin? She had never in her life felt so utterly helpless in the face of her own emotions. She couldn't even begin to describe her feelings when she thought of not sharing her life with him.

She entered Justin's office at eleven o'clock, the thick portfolio under her arm and steely determination in her eyes. At least her survey—all neatly assembled and analyzed—was worthy of pride.

Marie greeted her with a wide, toothy smile. "Welcome back, stranger. Where's my bottle of clean air?"

Leslie smiled back and shook her head. "I failed you, Marie, I'm sorry."

"Well . . ." she prodded, "are the natives up there just as willing to talk about themselves as they are here, or—" The door behind her opened and Justin's elegant silver-maned head peered out.

"Can you spare Leslie for a while?" he asked with gentle irony.

Leslie sat in her chair watching Justin's face as he pored over her report. At last he looked up, peering over his reading glasses at her. "Excellent. You didn't let me down."

An hour later they were having lunch together in a corner booth at Musso and Frank's restaurant on Hollywood Boulevard. "Well," Justin said offhandedly, "are you ready to hear my offer?"

Leslie caught her breath and nodded.

"Your new job will mean moving, I'm afraid. You won't have all the bright lights of L.A., but then you'll have the challenge of setting up your own office and having several teams in the field at all times. I'll send Marie up to help you organize the office for the first few weeks. Just on loan. She'll be thrilled."

Her heart was racing from the buildup of tension. "Don't do this to me, Justin. Where is it?"

"Oh, didn't I say?" He looked innocently at her. "Santa Barbara, of course. From Santa Maria on the north to Ventura on the south—rather a big territory. The board has been waiting for the right person, and I convinced them to take a chance on you."

Leslie's hand was shaking as she set down her cup of tea. Her mind was racing. "Why didn't *you* take it?" She couldn't believe what he had just offered her.

"I'd miss the Music Center, the theaters, all my old cronies here at Musso's. It's something you should think about, as well. Santa Barbara may be too tame for a woman with your energy."

"No," she almost shouted, "it won't be. I'll love it." She felt positively giddy. "When?"

He smiled at her faltering composure. "Is next month too soon? We're negotiating for office space in Santa

Barbara right now. You had me worried when you came home early from your project. I thought you'd decided to accept your young man's proposal and go away with him to Italy."

Leslie leaned forward. "I'm not going anywhere but Santa Barbara. You already gave me a fabulous team, and I'll do the best job anyone's ever done, I promise!"

He patted her hand and grinned. "Of course you will. Now eat your Cobb salad. Olson and Loeb don't like emaciated branch managers." He signaled to the waiter for more of the warm sourdough bread.

Too restless to go back to her apartment, Leslie drove out to Santa Monica beach and walked on the cool sand just above the edge of the placid wavelets of low tide. Santa Barbara! She couldn't quite believe it. This meant that she would have all the time in the world with Greg, time to move slowly. Perfect. Her heart was almost bursting.

Ahead of her, if she kept on walking, was Santa Barbara, and somewhere there was a little apartment waiting for her. It seemed as if everything she could dream of was hers now, on her terms. Not headlong and off balance. Just absolutely right.

Saturday morning, with nothing planned for the long weekend, Leslie found herself picking up the telephone and calling the Seaview Inn. There was such a thing as false pride. She'd realized that was what had been keeping her from being the first one to break the awful silence between them.

Ofelia answered the phone. "Señor Austin is in Philadelphia with Davy. Didn't you know?"

Leslie's heart sank. "They weren't supposed to go for another week. What happened?"

"The judge change the day," Ofelia told her.

"When is the custody hearing?" asked Leslie patiently.

"Monday morning. They cannot take Davy from us . . ." Ofelia's voice cracked.

"Listen, Ofelia, we can't help them by worrying. Why don't you plan one of your best Mexican dinners for them when they get back—"

"*If* they get back. I could not even say *adiós* to Davy yesterday. I did not want him to see tears on my face, you know?"

Leslie felt the intensity of Ofelia's grief. "When are they due back—Monday night?"

"*Sí,*" she responded.

"Then set an extra place for me. I want to be there when all the hugs and kisses start." She hoped she sounded sure of herself.

"You are a very nice lady," Ofelia said. "You make people feel better, you know? This old house feels empty to me, even with two guests staying here. It's not the same. . . ."

"Did Davy ever do his show-and-tell at school with his acorns?" Leslie asked to lighten the mood.

"He give the best report of all. The teacher give him grade A."

"I'll bet Roger Cranston was jealous."

Ofelia laughed, sounding more like her cozy self. Leslie heard the grandfather clock bonging in the background, and then the stately Westminster chimes. "We miss you," Ofelia said, "all of us."

"I miss all of you," Leslie replied. "But not for long. I'm going to be your neighbor. My company is making me the manager of its new office in Santa Barbara, starting next month."

"Ah, *señorita*," she breathed warmly, "this will be so good for him. He has such a terrible time with his heart."

"Hearts are hard for everyone," she said, side-stepping Ofelia's gambit. "By the way, I think I left a little tape recorder in my room. I'll pick it up on Monday, if you find it."

"I have not seen it, but I will look. Ah, *señorita*, I could give you a big *abrazo*. The Holy Mother has sent you into our life, I know this." Leslie could almost hear the rustling of Ofelia crossing herself against her ample bosom.

"We'll have lots of time for everything, including your teaching me how to cook those incredible enchiladas. Now stop worrying and believe that Davy will be on that plane Monday night."

She agreed. "I have promise to God I will never get mad at Davy again if he let him come home to us."

Leslie hung up, feeling as if she had touched the meaning of home for a moment, with its earthy mixture of love and anxiety, tears and joy. Home wasn't perfection; it was light and shadow and textures, and challenges that forced everyone to grow.

She pulled on her denim skirt and oversize lavender cotton sweater and drove to a place she had never thought of visiting before she met Greg Austin—the Southwest Museum, with its famous collection of Native American art and artifacts. She didn't want to stew alone in her apartment, mirroring Greg's emotions wherever he was in Philadelphia. It wouldn't have helped to tell Ofelia the truth, that she was just as worried that Davy might be lost to them.

Leslie was almost alone in her wanderings through the rooms of the museum, which were silent yet full of faraway voices connected with the beautiful baskets, painted bowls, and evidence of the everyday life of American Indians. On her way out she browsed in the gift shop, picking up a book on the Chumash painted caves.

An hour later, as Leslie drove up to her apartment complex, she noticed Derek's silver BMW pulling away from the curb. She entered the apartment lobby through the garage access door and found an envelope shoved partway into her mail slot.

With annoyance already rising in her she quickly opened the envelope. "Leslie," it read in neat typing, "considering our status, I would very much appreciate your returning my house key at once. One doesn't want to invite problems by having keys in too many hands. D." That was all, not even a handwritten signature. True to his meticulous nature he had enclosed a self-addressed stamped envelope.

All day Sunday, Leslie immersed herself in paperwork. She sat at the dining room table, studying the thick pile of management guidelines Justin had given her on Friday. It was well after midnight when she allowed herself the luxury of rest and finally went to bed, too tired to think.

She was jolted out of a deep sleep by the insistent ringing of the telephone next to her bed. "This is ridiculous," she muttered, groping for the receiver, wishing she'd unplugged it last night.

"Hel—"

"Les, thank God you're there!" Greg's breathless voice reached her ear. "Listen, I don't have much time—"

"Greg?" she asked, not quite alert. "What time is it? It's the middle of the—"

"Ten o'clock in the morning here in Philadelphia. Now listen to me, please! The whole case may fall apart. It's hanging on the issue of our home life. The lawyers are making me sound like some California hippie who runs a crash pad by the beach. They've just finished dredging up old history about Celeste's death, and the way I took Davy away from the Hartshorns They called it kidnapping. I'm scared to death—"

"Stop a second," Leslie interjected.

"I'm having the devil's own time with my temper," he continued through her words, "but I won a ten-minute recess. Les, I beg you, help me. I'll make it all up to you someday."

"What do you mean?" Her senses were suddenly sharp.

"Marry me, Les. Right away. It's the only way I'll walk out of here with Davy."

"Greg, stop a second..." She couldn't quite believe this was happening.

"The old dragons who came to the inn said you seemed to be a responsible person, and maybe I was wrong to give the judge the idea that we were engaged. But dear God, Les, I was desperate! Celeste's parents are sitting there like a pair of vultures. It's worse than I thought. I know I have no right to ask like this. Les . . . Les? Are you still there?"

There was a long silence on the line while Leslie waged war with her pride and emotions. "Does Davy approve of this?" she asked finally.

"He loves you, you know that." Greg's frantic urgency reached through the phone to her, and she saw her joyfully conceived plans crumbling at her feet.

"What do you want me to say?" she whispered.

"The magic word in this crazy scenario is *wife*. Will you do it, Les?"

"Marry in haste, repent at leisure," she replied sardonically.

"We can work everything else out when we come to it. I wouldn't ask if I didn't love you, believe me. We would have gotten married sooner or later, anyway."

"Don't say another word," Leslie warned. "You aren't making it any better." She could hear Derek's voice saying almost the same words to her. "Just tell Davy...tell him I love him, too, and everything's going to be all right."

"You mean you'll do it?"

"Do I have a choice?"

"Honest, Les, if there were any other way. . ."

Leslie was silent again, resenting the easy way he'd told her he loved her. "When is the happy occasion?"

"I'd like to tell the judge it'll be soon—like a week."

"Then what are you standing around talking for? Go tell the judge you've got a new mom for Davy. And give Davy a hug for me."

"Les . . . if there were any other way, I—"

She hung up the phone slowly, deliberately, while Greg was still apologizing to her.

13

LESLIE LAY BACK in her bed. "What a rotten mess," she said into the empty room. Life wasn't playing fair. First Derek wanted to marry her so he could be a partner in his law firm . . . and now this. What did that make her, she brooded darkly.

She would marry Greg—she loved Davy, too—but she wouldn't have Greg pretending she was the woman of his dreams. He was just the kind of emotional man who'd mistake gratitude for love, and there must be none of that. She'd rather have him honestly admit that she was more or less Davy's unpaid nursemaid.

There would be a lot to set straight in the next few days if he expected to have a wedding.

The little apartment was dense with imaginary conversations, serious discussions between herself and Greg about Davy, about life, about marriage. She came at the problems from every angle, anticipating Greg's point of view, analyzing her own, trying to find some ultimate, beautiful logic in what they were about to do.

When at last she felt she could handle it, she called Justin and told him she was getting married and why. "It's something I have to do," she added when Justin didn't comment at first.

"Do I understand this correctly?" he asked slowly. "You're not marrying the young man who wanted to take you to Italy, but you *are* marrying a man you've known for less than two weeks."

"I didn't expect it to sound reasonable, Justin, but I've made my decision and I'll stick with it."

"Why do I feel you're uncomfortable, then?"

"Don't ask me more, Justin. I'm doing the best I can under the circumstances."

"I have yet to hear the word *love* in any of this. Is something wrong with my hearing?" he chided.

"There's love, it's just buried deep. Greg and I will have to find it, that's all."

She heard a sigh on the other end of the line. "So you're going to be living at this little inn of his?"

"I'm not sure," she replied. That was something she hadn't figured out yet.

"One piece of advice from an old warrior," he said seriously. "Don't do anything halfway. You'll never be satisfied unless you give it all you've got. Then if it fails, you have no regrets. That goes for life experiences in all their myriad forms."

"Thanks, Justin."

"Just keep me posted. Olson and Loeb mustn't think I've given you too long a leash. Bless you both."

"One more thing," she said.

"Yes . . ." he intoned warily.

"I've been studying the management guidelines and I'm more confident than ever that I'll make you proud of me with the new office."

"You're a remarkable woman, Leslie, remarkable."
He ended with a little chuckle.

Leslie wrote a letter informing her landlord of her
departure, then went to the post office and made out a
change of address form, rerouting her mail to Justin's
office until she knew where she would be living in Santa
Barbara. Keeping busy she could almost avoid thinking about her next meeting with Greg. By midafter-
noon she still hadn't decided whether to drive to Santa
Barbara for the homecoming welcome.

Ofelia solved the problem by calling the apartment
with the news that Greg and Davy were coming into
L.A. international airport at five o'clock. "I think it is
good if you meet them," she suggested, "and then you
all together come home. Davy will be so tired if they
take the bus."

"Sure," Leslie said. "We should be in Santa Barbara
by seven."

She stood in the American Airlines arrival lounge
feeling more nervous by the moment as the passengers
started streaming from the plane. Davy broke from the
crowd and ran toward her with his arms outstretched.

"We did it!" he shouted and threw his little body
against hers. "We did it!"

"I knew you would," she said, choking back tears.
When she looked up, Greg was very close, waiting for
her to see him.

"We did it," he echoed in a rough whisper, "thanks
to you."

Leslie took Davy's hand and tried to sound natural.
"I'm glad you're both back. It must have been hard."

She didn't look at Greg as she spoke. "Ofelia's making a welcome-home dinner and she called me at the last minute to come pick you up. She thought you'd all be tired, so..."

She felt Greg's hand on her arm, firm and urgent, stopping her determined forward motion. He turned her to face him. There was pain in his dappled green eyes and his lips moved slightly, but he said nothing. Then she saw that he was fighting down his own tears. "Oh, Les," he said, "I..."

"You don't have to say anything. Let's just get everyone home and then we can talk. I mean it," she said determinedly. "I don't want to discuss our future while we're in the middle of LAX. Give me that amount of space, please."

Greg backed away. "Right," he said quickly and looked down at Davy. "Let's go, *compadre*. Ofelia's got a batch of hot tortillas waiting."

Davy flashed a grin at Leslie. "Don't ever bother goin' to Phila... Philadelphia. It's awful."

"How come?" she asked as they neared the baggage claim area.

He shrugged his shoulders. "They don't know nothin' about the Chumash Indians."

For the first time Leslie laughed, then Greg joined in and all three of them shared the joke. Leslie realized how hard it was going to be to resist being drawn too fast into the warm vibration of family.

At seven o'clock exactly Leslie's car pulled up to the front door of the Seaview Inn. Ofelia raced down the steps and swept Davy against her body until he was almost lost in the folds of her flowered apron. "Davy, *mijo!*" she chanted again and again. Greg opened his arms wide enough to embrace them both.

"Your prayers must have worked," he said earnestly. "I was never a believer, but I am now." He kissed Ofelia gently on one cheek and got a big, teary kiss in return.

"Let's eat now," she ordered. "You, too, *señorita.* Everybody a big happy family again, *sí?*" Her dark eyes glistened with emotion.

Dinner was agony. Feelings that Leslie had held at bay with her logical mind were flooding back. Yearnings were torturing her as she sat so near to Greg, while everyone talked a mile a minute about the court case.

"Señor Vargas was going to be here tonight, but his wife start to have her baby today," Ofelia said. "Marriage is good for a man."

"Dad's gonna marry Leslie," Davy said, as if on cue. "I made 'em promise I could tell you."

She crossed herself twice in succession. "*¡Madre mía!* Is true?" she demanded, looking first at Greg and then at Leslie.

"It's true," Leslie said.

Ofelia sat back in her chair like a huge rag doll.

"They're gonna get married on Saturday, Dad says." Leslie shot Greg a look. "Saturday?"

He cleared his throat and stood up. "That's one of the things we have to arrange. Maybe we should take a walk. Excuse us, everyone. Davy, get ready for bed and I'll be up in a while to say good-night."

"Take plenty time," Ofelia said with a wink.

Leslie said nothing as they left the dining room and went outside. Greg had taken her hand, and the sensation was devastating. The old electricity was back, as if nothing had changed since that night on the leaf-strewn boulder.

He led her into the little gazebo in the side garden, then took her into his arms and held her. "I don't know what to say, Les," he whispered close to her ear. "Whatever you think of me, I want you to believe that I love you."

Leslie stiffened and pulled back. "Don't use that word with me, Greg. It isn't fair. We both know why I'm here and it doesn't deserve the word *love*. A better term is arrangement."

Greg looked at her stubborn face—the defiant set of her mouth, the challenging eyes. "You're wrong, but I'll have to convince you. I can see that."

"Don't try humoring me. I—"

Her words were suddenly stopped by the pressure of his mouth over hers. She couldn't escape his firm embrace because her back was against the latticework of the garden house. An involuntary moan escaped her as her resistance faltered and she eagerly responded to his ardor.

When she could breathe again she kissed his ear and said, "This has nothing to do with our marriage, Greg."

She felt him shudder with pleasure. "Of course not. I just didn't want us to forget what we once had. Care to join me in the tower?"

"On one condition," she managed to say, as he slid his hand up under the soft give of her sweater and found her breast. "This is simple animal passion, nothing more. We don't call it love."

"Whatever you say," he groaned as her hands cupped his buttocks and brought their thighs together. "We can't walk upstairs like this, can we?"

"I don't want you to stop touching me," she whispered.

"Oh, Les..." He brought her down gently to the wooden bench that was built against the gazebo wall. "The tower is too far."

"Hmm," she agreed, swiftly unbuttoning his flannel shirt to feel the fine mat of hair on his chest.

"WE STILL HAVE TO TALK," Greg whispered when their passion was finally spent. "I have to know what you're feeling."

"I know," she replied. "But not now, not here."

"You can have your old room back. Why don't we meet downstairs in the parlor in an hour? That's the proper place."

They straightened their clothing and walked back to the house hand in hand. They were both aware of Ofelia's face at the parlor window wreathed in an approving smile.

"We're still miles apart in understanding each other," Leslie said. She sat on the parlor love seat with Greg standing over her.

"I don't know what to say that will make you believe me," Greg protested for the second time during their awkward talk. "I would never marry someone just for convenience, not even to keep Davy. And I do love you, as feeble as that sounds right now."

Leslie nodded. "It does sound feeble. When did you start loving me, Greg—the minute the judge said you needed a wife?"

He turned his back for a moment and drew a deep breath. "I'm sorry for putting you through all this. We can get a quiet divorce after a reasonable time, if you want."

Leslie reached out to touch his arm. "That's not what I'm trying to say. We don't know what we want from a marriage. It would be idiotic to try to act as if this will be a true marriage. All I want is for us to keep a healthy distance while we get to know each other better."

"Better? Hellfire, woman! How much better is there!" he bellowed, then lost his steam and grinned. "You're right. So what if we're legally married? We're going to have a regulation-length courtship. Then, and only then, we'll have one hell of a honeymoon. Right?"

"Right. I want you to be so absolutely sure of me that you'll never even think I'd look at another man. And I have to be sure that you want me for myself."

"How could you look at another man when you have me?" he joked.

Leslie stood up and offered him her hand demurely. "Saturday will be fine for the wedding."

"Is the courthouse okay?"

"That will be fine. Now, it's late and I have to drive back early in the morning for a meeting with my boss. Starting next month I'm going to head up the newest branch of Olson and Loeb right here in Santa Barbara. I have a lot to do before Saturday."

A slow, wide smile creased the handsome face. "Everything's going right for both of us. And I couldn't be happier."

"Thanks. I'll leave it up to you to explain to Ofelia why I'll be sleeping in a separate bedroom, and why I'll be keeping my own name."

"That, too?" He looked a bit dashed.

"Those are my terms."

"Agreed," he said and kissed her hand gallantly before letting her go.

THE WEEK SPED BY. Justin held his tongue about Leslie's marriage plans; Marie thought it was terribly romantic. Leslie sent a telegram to her parents' cruise ship, breaking the news as gently as she could. *Poor Mother*, she mused. Derek would have been the perfect son-in-law for her. But Greg? Maybe he could win her over with sheer natural Western charm.

As Saturday neared, Leslie became more and more cheerful. No matter how determined she was to stand by the new rules of behavior, she was certain that she and Greg would work things out. If not for her inborn caution she'd have shouted to everyone around: I love him!

She arrived at the whitewashed Spanish-style courthouse just before three o'clock Saturday afternoon. Justin was there with Marie, and Jim Vargas was standing as Greg's best man. Ofelia had a handsome red-haired young man by her side.

Leslie had bought a cornflower-blue linen dress in a little shop on Wilshire Boulevard. She couldn't help wanting to appear beautiful, and the classic dress with its simple sheath lines and matching unstructured jacket was lovely. No matter what kind of wedding this was, it was hers and she was going to look like a bride, dammit. Her mood was a strange one as she walked toward the entrance to the building.

Greg met her with an armful of fresh flowers—roses from his garden—in pinks and sunrise colors. "I'm overwhelmed," he said softly, offering her his arm. She smiled, but it was difficult to keep up the appearance of calm. Inside, she was shaking like a leaf. She caught Justin's questioning eyes and tried to seem sure of herself.

The ceremony was short and warm, with the woman judge delivering a moving talk about faithfulness and mutual trust. There were tears in Leslie's eyes when she said I do. She didn't look up to see if there were tears in Greg's eyes, too.

Afterward, Jim Vargas hosted a wedding supper at the dining room of the El Encanto Hotel. The lovely Spanish hacienda was perched on a wooded hillside overlooking the city.

There were toasts all around, and very loving sentiments from the dear friends at the table. Then Greg rose with champagne glass in hand and lifted it toward his bride. "To the woman I love—a risk taker, a damned stubborn female and a constant challenge. To Leslie!"

Leslie could almost believe that his adoring look was genuine. Maybe he'd even deluded himself into thinking he loved her. Everyone was clapping and demanding to hear a word from the bride. Reluctantly, Leslie stood and tried to find something to say.

"Thank you all for being here. I needed you more than you think," she said. Laughter rippled around the table. "Since my parents are away, it was important to have my other family with me. My toast is to Greg, who is about to find out how much trouble he's gotten himself into by marrying me. To Greg!"

Greg caught her eye and smiled. He understood what she meant.

The good food and dancing extended into the evening. Finally, Justin excused himself and Marie. Jim kissed the bride and left to be with his own wife and newborn son, and Ofelia had to drag Davy from his second cup of hot chocolate.

"God bless you both," she said in a breaking voice. "I will come with Davy tomorrow morning and make a beautiful breakfast in bed, *sí*? Come, Davy, we stay tonight with my father."

When they were alone, Leslie said, "Breakfast in bed is going to be awkward. Didn't you tell Ofelia about our arrangement?"

Greg avoided her direct look. "I had trouble with that one, Les. She comes from a culture where the man is king. What would it do to my reputation if my wife slept in another room? We can tell her tomorrow. I'm sorry. She was so happy about us, and I didn't have the heart to tell her it wasn't the perfect marriage."

"It's got to be that way, Greg. We have to keep our promise."

"I do love you, Les," he said as he enveloped her hand in his.

"Not yet. Words are too easy. Can I have my old room, or is there somebody else sleeping there tonight?"

"I have it ready for you. I just didn't tell Ofelia who was reserving it. Shall we go home now, Mrs. Austin?"

"It's still Ms O'Neill."

He clicked his heels in a mock-military way. "Of course, Ms O'Neill. As you wish."

They kissed chastely at Leslie's bedroom door and said good-night. "I hope you're keeping a diary," Greg said, letting his tongue tip graze the outside of her lips. "Someday our grandchildren will want to know the real story of our romance."

"Don't count on grandchildren," she chided with a light touch of her finger against his chest. "Don't count on anything."

"You know where I'll be if you need anything . . . anything at all."

"You have no shame. Good night." She smiled in spite of herself and entered her room. It was like walking into a rose garden. Every available surface was covered with flowers, and her patchwork quilt was dappled with pink rose petals, strewn over the bed and across the floor. The fragrance was something out of a dream.

She noticed a small card tucked in among the largest of the bouquets beside the bed. "I promised I'd play by the rules, but I didn't promise I'd play fair. Love, Greg."

"Understood," she said. She was starting to feel very foolish. Bit by bit her wall of pride was starting to crumble. She sat on the edge of the bed, her whole being tuned to the maddeningly lovable man in the tower room, just a few steps away. How could she expect to sleep tonight or any other night? She paced the room, then stopped to look at herself in the tall mirror in the bathroom. *He hasn't satisfied your requirements for a husband*, she reminded the hopeful dark eyes that looked back at her. *You don't know, you can't be sure.*

She turned off the lamp beside the bed and slipped between the fine percale sheets. But instead of sinking into the enveloping softness of the down pillow, her cheek came down against something hard. She sat bolt upright and turned the light on again.

Her tape recorder! What was it doing there, and with a tape inside? She hadn't left a tape in it. She pressed the Play button. A flood of adrenaline raced through her body at the sound of Greg's whispering voice.

"My darling Les, it's seven-thirty and I miss you already. Whatever happens tonight with you and Derek, I have to tell you something. I can't seem to say things very well when we're face-to-face, but quite simply, I'm a hell of a long way into falling in love with you. That's all. Whatever you decide to do with your life, I want you to know I cared more than I could put into words. Love is a hard word to say."

Leslie rewound the tape and played it again. She was about to stop the machine when Greg's voice resumed.

"It's Thursday night and I still can't get you out of my system. Why did you have to leave me yesterday after you brought Davy back? You couldn't know the wrenching feeling in my gut when you walked away. . . and all I could do was stand there like an ass and tell you I needed you. Hell, Les, it's more than that. We're a team, dammit—an ornery, scrapping team that only comes along once in a lifetime. If you can't see that, I don't know what I'll do. Probably be celibate for the rest of my life. . . ."

Leslie smothered a laugh. *Celibate, my eye!* She could see his boyish face, all creased and tanned—and his earnest green eyes.

"Anyway," his voice continued seriously, "you've taken some rough edges off me that were way overdue for removal, believe it or not. You may not think so, but you've made me a better man.

"If I don't junk this tape, maybe someday you'll hear this and forgive me for making things so hard for you. I'm not dumb enough to think we'll get together again, but wouldn't it have been one wild and fantastic marriage?" The soft, deep voice broke, and then the tape was blank again.

Leslie stared at the little machine in her hand. She didn't need to play it back. Every word on the tape had been spoken before he went to Philadelphia. She knew what that meant. Her mind was racing now, reprogramming and rearranging all her assumptions.

All at once her idiotic pride dissolved. She was out of bed and moving toward the door as if a tremendous force was pulling her. Without even thinking of putting a robe over her satin nightgown, she left the room and raced down the main stairway and through the parlor, taking the tower steps two at a time. She stopped at Greg's door and knocked impatiently.

"Who is it?" the voice asked from within.

"The other half of the team, dammit. Let me in!"

"Who?" the teasing voice asked again.

"Leslie O'Neill-Austin. Mrs. Gregory Austin!"

"There's no such woman."

Leslie smiled to herself at the tantalizing game. "Beggin' your pardon, sir, but you're wrong," she said softly and turned the doorknob with a confident motion.

From out of the darkness Greg's sexy voice warned, "If you come near this bed I won't be responsible for the consequences, madam."

"You should have thought of that before you took me to the Botanic Gardens," Leslie whispered. She inhaled deeply of the pine scent near the shadowy bed and followed the magnetic pull until she was once again touching the wonderful body of her beloved husband.

Harlequin Temptation

COMING NEXT MONTH

HARLEQUIN HISTORICAL

Explore love with Harlequin in the Middle
Ages, the Renaissance, in the Regency, the
Victorian and other eras.

Relive within these books the endless ages of
romance, set against authentic historical
backgrounds. Two new historical love stories
published each month.

Take 4 best-selling love stories FREE
Plus get a FREE surprise gift!

What readers say about Harlequin Temptation...

One word is needed to describe the series Harlequin Temptation... "Exquisite." They are so sensual, passionate and beautifully written.

—H.D., Easton, PA

I'm always looking forward to the next month's Harlequin Temptation with a great deal of anticipation...

—M.B., Amarillo, TX

I'm so glad you now have Harlequin Temptation... the stories seem so real. They really stimulate my imagination!

—S.E.B., El Paso, TX

Names available on request.

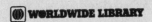

ATTRACTIVE, SPACE SAVING BOOK RACK

Display your most prized novels on this handsome and sturdy book rack. The hand-rubbed walnut finish will blend into your library decor with quiet elegance, providing a practical organizer for your favorite hard-or soft-covered books.

Only $9.95

Approximately 16" x 8" when assembled

Assembles in seconds!

To order, rush your name, address and zip code, along with a check or money order for $10.70* ($9.95 plus 75¢ postage and handling) payable to *Harlequin Reader Service*:

Harlequin Reader Service
Book Rack Offer
901 Fuhrmann Blvd.
P.O. Box 1325
Buffalo, NY 14269-1325

Offer not available in Canada.

*New York residents add appropriate sales tax.

BKR-1R